The GIRL from Himachal & Other Stories

The GIRL from Himachal
& Other Stories

Lt. Gen. Yashwant Mande

Ocean Books Pvt. Ltd.
ISO 9001:2015 Publishers

Published by

Ocean Books (P) Ltd.

4/19 Asaf Ali Road,
New Delhi-110 002 (INDIA)
e-mail: info@oceanbooks.in

ISBN 978-81-8430-110-6

The Girl from Himachal & Other Stories
by Lt. Gen. Yashwant Mande

Edition
2025

Price
₹ 300.00 (Rupees Three Hundred only)

Printed at
Yash Printographics, Noida

To
my wife
Banti

INTRODUCTION

I am grateful to the readers for their heartening response on my stories in the previous two books. It has encouraged me to continue with writing.

My first book, 'The Hero of Kargil & Other Stories' contained war stories which India has fought since Independence. The second book, 'The Terror in Kashmir & Other Stories' was on civil subjects, on different topics from Vedic period to the present times. This book contains stories on contemporary topics. The stories have been prompted by my experience of what I have seen, read, heard or thought about. There are three stories which are based on real lives, the remaining are imaginary.

The Girl from Himachal is based on the life of Samuel Evans Stokes. I had heard his name as pioneer who introduced apples to Himachal. It was later when I went into details that I learnt about his great contribution to our struggle for Independence and desire to identify himself with the people. His name is not known outside Himachal and I felt that the people in the rest of the country should know about him. Whatever I have written about him, his family and works are true; the plot and other characters are imaginary.

Godavari was my aunt, my mother's elder sister. Whatever she did is on the ground in the Central Hindu Girls School at Kammachha, Varanasi. She was called as 'Sister' and revered like lesser Malviya. She died when I was only thirteen year old; nevertheless she left indelible impression on my mind. I had to bring her back to life and I am glad that I have been able to write a story on her. The incidence at Chitrakoot and a few other episodes are imaginary. By large the story is a true reflection of her life and achievements.

Shanta Babu is a story based on the life of Shantaram Nagarkar, a very admirable character. He played good hockey and was a noble person. I had spent my childhood in Gorakhpur and I knew him. I lost contact with him when I joined army at the age of sixteen. The story is based on his life but it is not factual like biography. Fiction part has been added to make the story interesting.

The stories are meant for entertainment and literature is a superior pastime. I have no intention to be didactic or teach moral values but if the stories do, it is incidental. I must state that at the back of my mind are Matthew Arnold's views; the writers should spread good things of life. Here, I would like to mention that the best stories ever written are those from Ramayana and Mahabharata. They are interesting and at the same time educative.

It is heartening to note the progress made by women in our country. They are in every field of activity; you can see them in the offices, banks, malls and all places of work. They are successfully managing high offices and accepting difficult assignments in the armed forces and the police. They have done proud to the country in sports. The key to the progress of our country lies in their uplift and giving them equal share. Half of the stories in this book are devoted to women.

In writing these stories, I gratefully acknowledge the help given to me by Major General K.S. Pendse (Retd). He has been giving me inspiration to write and has been doing the onerous work of editing. Keshav is a widely read intellectual and a storehouse of knowledge. His suggestions and advises have helped me a great deal.

—Yashwant Mande

January 2011

CONTENTS

THE GIRL FROM HIMACHAL

The bungalow next to mine was owned by a lady whose son and daughter were working in America. She was going to the US and wanted to rent out her house for two years. She preferred students as tenants for timely vacation; she was able to hire the upper portion to a student and was looking forward to a similar arrangement for the lower part, which had the facility of a garden and an open space.

One morning, when I was sitting outside in my lawn, I saw a middle aged couple with a fair, good looking girl. She had come to Pune for doing MBA from Symbiosis College. She could not get hostel accommodation. She spent first two months in a flat sharing a room with other girls. She didn't like the arrangement and was fed up.

Two days later my neighbour with the new tenant came to my house and told me about their deal to rent out the lower portion. She told me that she was leaving that very night for the US and reminded me about looking after the house in her absence.

The tenants introduced themselves as Mr. and Mrs. Parmar. They appeared to be a decent couple. They agreed to pay the stipulated rent as also to employ the existing servants i.e. the cook, *mali*[1] and the maid. The Parmars were happy with the

---

1. Gardener.

new arrangement; the college for their daughter was not far off and the house was an ongoing affair with all facilities. The only thing left for them was to buy a scooter for their daughter to move around.

Mrs. Parmar said that her daughter was not used to living in flats and sharing room with others. Life in Himachal is so different from the crowded cities; she was glad that she had found a suitable place for her daughter. She asked me if I had been to Himachal.

I told them that I had an army background. I had served in Punjab for many years and from there I had visited all reputed hill stations in Himachal. They were pleased to know about my service in uniform. Mr Parmar said that he had a few relatives in the army; I knew two of them. They stayed for a week and went back. Before going, Suresh Parmar told me that his daughter was young, just 22 years in age, but she was a bold girl with certain ambitions to fulfil; nonetheless he would be relying on me for the safety of their daughter.

Parmars were new to Pune. They did not have any friends or relatives in the place. Suresh came to my house several times to chit chat and spend time. As a retired man I had all the time and I found his company likeable. Their family had acquired money in apple business. He was not rich like businessmen of big cities who have no time to themselves and no other interest. Plantation requires a different kind of aptitude and they follow the life style of agricultural community.

Once during his visit, Suresh told me about the history of apple plantation in Himachal Pradesh. Samuel Evans Stokes was an American from Philadelphia born with a missionary zeal. He came to India in 1904 at the age of 21 to serve with an organisation dedicated to fight leprosy. From America he brought saplings of Golden Delicious and Red Delicious apples. These were planted in his orchard and the first crop was ready in 1926.

The apples became a hit in the Indian market because of

their sweet taste and pleasing appearance. Prior to these, apples were grown in Kullu and Manali but they were sour. The country imported sweet varieties of apples from Japan. The new varieties were an immense success, so much so that the import from Japan stopped completely.

Samuel Stokes belonged to a rich family. They were owners of a prosperous elevator manufacturing company. His mother, Florence, wanted him to return and take over the charge of the business. But Samuel was least interested in business and was determined to follow his ideals. He identified himself with the local people and lived like them His mother finally gave up and came to India herself in 1911 to meet her son. She purchased 200 acres of land for her son to start an apple plantation and sent him a consignment of delicious apple saplings. That was the beginning of apple plantation and since then apples have proliferated all over in Himachal and as on date, the state has become No 1 producer of apples in the country."

"That's interesting. I didn't know this part," I said.

"The contribution made by Samuel Stokes was much greater. Not many in our country know that he was the first foreigner, an American who fought for the Independence of our country. He was jailed in Lahore by the British for his activities and inflammatory speeches.

He liked Indian culture for its simplicity and embraced Hindu religion. He changed his name to Satyanand. He married a Rajput-Christian girl in 1912.

Satyanand Stokes was deeply impressed by the Indian philosophy and learned Sanskrit. He built a temple next to his house at Barobagh. The panels of the temple depict inscriptions from Gita and Upanishads.

He died in the year 1946. His children followed his footsteps. Vidya Stokes is well known. She was president of the Pradesh Congress Party and the speaker of the legislative assembly."

I apologised to Suresh Parmar about my ignorance. I had been to Himachal many times and yet I did not know anything about this great man.

"That is OK," he said. "India is such a big country. It is difficult for people from one part to know the happenings in other states, but for us he was an angel and we will remember him forever. The apple growers are heavily indebted to him.

I must tell you that my daughter Rati is inspired by his example. The apple plantation requires manual labour and they have not benefitted much. She wants to do something for them, put them on par with industrial labour and that's why she wants to learn business administration."

I told Suresh, "I am happy to hear that. Be assured that I will look after your daughter. And yes, one thing more, next time when we go to Himachal, we would like to visit the place where Satyanand Stokes lived and worked."

Rati was a sweet girl with sharp features. Her eyes were big and attractive, and the dimple on her cheek became prominent whenever she smiled. As a rule she used to come to our house for meals on Sundays. This routine stopped after three months, apparently she had made enough friends by that time and obviously she liked the company of her own age group.

Madan Modi was the boy who lived upstairs. He came from a renowned industrial family of Mumbai. He was senior to Rati by two years, handsome, sharp and smart. He was not very interested in studies and attendance. He used to tell his friends, "There is nothing much in what they teach us in the college, I know these things by virtue of living in the business house environment."

Madan was an extrovert and a good social mixer. He spent most of his time in cultivating acquaintance with people in high places. His father was happy with his ability to make contacts and made use of him for promoting his business in Pune. Money was sent to him whenever he required, meals were sent to him frequently from Mumbai and whenever he went to his house, he returned with a new brand of car.

Living in the same bungalow acquaintance was natural which soon turned into friendship and then intimacy. They fell in love and expressed their resolve for lifelong partnership. Madan took her to the best of places in the city, nearby hills and holiday resorts. Rati was dazzled by exquisite things of life, expensive hotels, grandeur of the Western coast and exotic beaches. Age was with them and they enjoyed every moment of being together in love.

Madan introduced her to his friends and twice he took her to Mumbai to meet his parents. My neighbour's house had become active, as never before, for evening get together and parties.

The locality of Anand Park had its share of retired people, very inquisitive and observant. Madan and Rati had become a topic for gossip. Rati had two facets; one of the simple college going girl in ordinary attire and the other of mod-mod, sophisticated girl in latest costumes and make up for the evenings. She looked beautiful like a model. The elderly crowd called her Heart-Throb and that she was. They pestered me with all kinds of questions, the most common being- are they going to get married and if so when? I wish I could answer their questions; the fact was that Rati had stopped meeting us.

Madan and Rati had spent several months in love. It was the month of February, a month before the commencement of examinations. It occurred to them that they would have to concentrate on studies. They decided to host a gala party before setting their mind on intensive studies.

The house was decorated with festoons and coloured lights. Madan had hired the best jazz band and given contract for lavish dinner. The guests started pouring in from 8 P.M. onwards. The street was lined on both sides with cars and motorcycles and the lawn was crowded, mostly with young boys and girls. The music was playing on loud pitch and the youngsters were singing and dancing in gay abandon. It was the most noisy and gorgeous party that I had seen in Anand Park.

Madan and Rati had invited us for the party but sixth sense prevailed and we did not go. We would have been out of place with the young crowd but we were watching them dancing and singing from the lawn of our house. It was past midnight when the party came to an abrupt end. The mobile squad of the police had reached questioning the host for playing loud music beyond 9.30 P.M. in a residential area. The guests departed in a hurry. The police grilled Madan and Rati for violating the rule. All that they could tell the police was their reason for throwing the party before they got down to serious studies and ignorance of law. Madan was taken to the police station for recording his statement leaving Rati alone in the house.

It was 4 o'clock in the morning when Madan returned from the police station. Rati was feeling nervous. They sipped coffee to cool down. Little did they know that the consequences of the party would be disastrous.

Madan's family was well known. The police sent a copy of the report to his father marked as confidential. They also mentioned about his affair with a girl which was bringing disrepute to their family. Madan's father took prompt action. The boy was called to Mumbai and within a week he was sent on a business tour to Australia and New Zealand. Madan protested saying that he was in love with the girl and wanted to marry her.

"That is something new to me. You never told me that before!"

"I didn't but you have seen the girl. Is anything wrong with her?"

"I have nothing to comment on the girl but you cannot marry her."

"Why?"

"Look, marriages don't take place because of infatuation. You must understand that you belong to an industrial house and therefore, you have to marry a girl from another business family as that would enhance our assets and influence. In our occupation money counts; without money we have no meaning, with money we have everything. We can influence politicians, bureaucrats, police and exercise control on whole lot of our employees. As you grow up you would realise that you have responsibilities to fulfil, do some meaningful work and not spend your time in love and frolics. You should also realise that at 24 you are too young to marry."

Madan was deeply upset. He was comforted by his mother and other ladies in the house. He understood that he had responsibilities to fulfil and he was too young for marriage. But where was the hurry? The marriage could wait. Why should marriage interfere with work? He could not turn back from his words. What would Rati think of him?

His mother was tactful. She told him that she was glad that he accepted that he was too young for marriage and that he would have to wait. "Has it occurred to you that the parents of the girl may object? People in our country are orthodox and they do not approve inter-caste marriages. Don't take it for granted that they will agree just because you are from a rich family. From little that I know Parmars are Rajput and they are very rigid. Have you checked this aspect from the parents of the girl?"

"No."

"Then do that first. Meanwhile you must go on the foreign trip as that is connected with work and duty. You can always talk to the girl on telephone."

Madan told Rati about the developments in Mumbai and his going abroad. From Australia he used to ring her every day. As the time passed the frequency of his call came down and to his dismay he found that the response from his sweetheart was cooling down.

From his childhood Madan was used to a life of comfort. He got whatever he wanted. Australia is an expensive country but even there, there was no shortage of money for him. Because of sheer habits he used to frequent the best places of entertainment. He realised what his father had said, we would be nowhere if we did not have money. By nature he was lusty;

he remembered Rati for sometime but thereafter gave in to sexual urge. The other girls were as good.

After three months of stay in Australia and New Zealand, Madan was sent to America for one year. By that time he had got tuned to the industrial culture of the West. He saw the light of his father's views; the most important thing in life was to make money, the other things were of secondary significance. The memories of his love for Rati were getting obliterated. He was doing well in the various assignments given to him and that made his father happy.

Rati had got down to serious studies. She had neglected books for many months and she had to make up. She got annoyed with Madan when he asked her to ascertain consent from her parents. She told him that they never asked the permission of their parents when they fell in love, why had that become necessary now? Why didn't this requirement enter into his mind before indulging in intimacies? And how would that matter if they were resolved to get married? She called him a coward. She decided to forget her affair with him and was quite happy when the calls stopped.

Once during her examination days she came to our house. She said that her elder brother would be coming in a fortnight's time to take her back home. She requested me and my wife to keep her affair with Madan as secret and not to disclose anything to her brother.

Rati took precautions to ensure that her brother did not meet anyone in the locality. He stayed for a week in Pune and Rati kept him occupied showing him various sight-seeing places in the city and around.

The gossip mongers of Anand Park were taken by surprise. Who was this new entry that the Heart Throb had enticed? The new face was more intriguing because he stayed with her in the same lower portion of the house. I was showered with questions. I told my fellow dwellers that he was her brother. Apparently my reply did not satisfy their curiosity. One of them asked me if I had met her brother. When I said 'No', he gave a mischievous smile. Another was quick to say, "The modern girls are clever; they know how to deal with situations." And yet another remarked, "When one goes, the other walks in. That's the lifestyle of modern girls."

Rati came back after the summer vacation. This time she travelled alone flying from Delhi to Pune. She picked up the keys from our house and moved into the bungalow. The servants were waiting for her return and she had no problem in settling down. The upper portion remained vacant.

The months were passing by. Rati remained aloof occupied in her studies. Many of Madan's friends knew her and they tried to make contact. She spurned them and did not allow visitors to enter the house. There was a noticeable change and the pensioner's lot in the colony were astonished to observe the dramatic change.

Rati had started visiting our house once in a while. On one occasion I asked her about Madan. She said that the chapter was closed. She acknowledged that it was her fault. They had no previous knowledge of each other and the family background. What she did was a blunder, something like a love affair of strangers meeting in a hotel. She possibly could not have fitted in a *Marwari*[1] family decked in jewels and ornaments, and nothing else to do. She had an ambition in her life of being an active girl working for the poor. She was convinced that it was a most stupid case of love but it did happen. She fell a victim to temptations and thanked God for recovering in time.

The second year for Rati was without any deviation from studies and she was doing extremely well. After the examination, Suresh Parmar and his wife came to Pune to take their daughter back to Himachal. They were good tenants; Suresh insisted that I must check the house to make sure that it has been vacated in good condition. He thanked me for looking after his daughter.

---

1. Business Community.

Before leaving he asked me, "When are you coming to Himachal?"

"Next year," I said. "This time I would like to visit the work place of Satyanand Stokes."

"That won't pose any problem."

My neighbour, Mrs Gadkari was back from the trip to US. She was most pleased, the rent was paid in full and the house was vacated in good time before her arrival.

I had an understanding with my neighbour to look after each other's house whenever one of us moved out. It was now her turn as we were going to Himachal.

I was not new to Simla and other hill stations in Himachal. From Punjab I had been visiting these stations on work cum holidays. The weather in the hills was cool and invigorating, most welcome during summer months. One must thank the British for developing hill stations in various parts of the country. Simla was called the queen of the hill stations and had the privilege of becoming the summer capital of India. The Viceroy with his secretariat and commander in chief used to come here every year. The drill for movement of the capital was meticulously worked out. Delhi was connected by a broad gauge railway line up to Kalka and thereafter a narrow gauge line carried people and stores right up to Simla. The journey in the slow match box train was pleasant and exciting; specially designed stops were made for breakfast and lunch catering to the requirements of *Bara Sahibs*[1]. Those were different days; the lifestyle was easy with plenty of leisure time for hobbies and pursuits, one could read books and enjoy poetry. There was hardly any habitation between Ambala and Kalka, and Chandigarh did not exist. Since then the situation has changed; the crowd in Simla mall rub against each other and no avenue is available for peaceful walks. Simla is overcrowded, disturbing peace and solitude.

---

1. British officers.

Himachal is a mountainous state; its share of plains territory is negligible. Simla has a name but there are a large number of hill stations and resorts spread out on road from Kalka to Simla and beyond, and the road from Dharamsala to Kullu-Manali. The state has a long history from the Vedic period. It has the reputation of being known as *Dev Bhoomi*[1] and has tremendous potential for development.

We had spent a month in Kasauli. It is nearest from Kalka, a military station providing holiday home facilities to retired officers. It is a peaceful place, a pensioner's paradise.

I had not forgotten the purpose of my visit. I wanted to know all about Satyanand Stokes. After a month we went to Simla and met Suresh Parmar. Their family is well known and they have their bungalow away from city centre on NH 22. I told Suresh about my keenness to visit the place where Samuel Stokes lived. He smiled, "I had told you that it would not be difficult. Right now Rati is staying there and she will tell you all about that great man."

We left Simla in the morning and reached Kufri after two hours. The place is famous for snowfall and attracts people during winters. It has facility for skating and winter sports. We stopped there for a cup of tea.

From Kufri we continued our journey on the highway and reached Narkanda. It is a market town for apples. From here, the national highway goes to Rampur and beyond to borders with China. We saw convoys of army vehicles carrying personnel and stores to their destination, known as Sugar Sector.

A narrow road from Narkanda goes to Thanedar, Kotgarh and then to Tibet. It was the old pilgrim's route to Mansarover and Kailash when NH 22 did not exist. This was the route which we took and our destination was Thanedar, a place intimately linked with Samuel Stokes.

Thanedar is a beautiful place. Rudyard Kipling called it as 'Mistress of the Northern Hills.' Rati met us here and made

---

1. The abode of Gods.

arrangements for our stay. We were delighted to meet her and could not have hoped for a better guide. Rati was a changed girl, clad in *khadi*[1] and looked much like the locals.

Rati took us to the bungalow built by Samuel Evans Stokes. It is a two storied structure constructed on top of a hillock and is known as 'Harmony Hall.' From here one could see the Himalayan snow covered peaks on three sides. The immediate impression is that of total peace, solitude and harmony. No wonder Samuel Stokes decided to settle down here permanently.

We then went to the temple built by him after his conversion to Hinduism in 1937. It is called as Paramjyoti Mandir. J.K. Birla had sent him a cheque of Rs 20,000/- to help him for construction of the temple. The Birla House is known for giving generous help for the religious cause and that tradition continues to this date. The temple is Satyanand's gift to the people of Thanedar. On the walls of the temple, verses are inscribed from Upanishads and Gita which inspired him and will do so for many others in times to come.

Next day Rati took us to Kotgarh, 6 kms away. The attraction of this place is an old church built by the British in 1843. Its importance lies in shaping the mind of Samuel Stokes. He could not bear the heat of Punjab and was sent here for rest and recuperation in May 1904. He spent his time in meeting people and pilgrims going to Mansarovar and Kailash. He went on long treks in the mountains. He fell in love with the place and decided to live his life in the hills. It was here that the suitability of the area for apple plantation took root in his mind.

On return to Thanedar, Rati gave us two books on Satyanand. "My father has already told you about him in Pune, you have visited the place and seen for yourself and here are books which will give more knowledge and information."

"What have you learnt from him?" I asked.

Rati blushed. "I have learnt to distinguish between good and pleasant."

---

1. Hand spun and woven cotton fabric.

"I don't understand you?"

She said, "I am not competent to explain these matters. The *Purohit*[1] in the temple is a learned man in scriptures and the right person to talk to."

"I certainly would talk to him on this and many more matters but there is something which I want to know from you. Tell me is that the reason why you discarded Madan?"

She looked down and muttered, "yes."

The next two days were spent in going to the temple. Purohit was an elderly man. He had seen Satyanand Stokes in his childhood and had learnt a great deal about him from his father, who was in charge of the temple at that time.

"Our scriptures, Upanishads and Gita are in the form of verses. No detailed explanation is given as it could not have been done in those days. But the directions are clear and it leads one to think further on paramount problems of life. Take for example this verse, 'The good and pleasant are two different things.' We know it and yet we confuse between the two and sooner or later repent. Now, the pleasant things cannot be denied. Food, shelter, clothes, sex, rest etc are pleasant and essential, but they cannot be an end in themselves. Good is something which lies beyond. A large number of people get addicted to alcohol, tobacco and women because it pleases their sense organs. But, are they good? We fall victim to temptations and crudest form of hedonism. We damage ourselves and are no good to others.

In another Upanishad it is said, 'Take that much as you need, the rest belongs to society.' Now, we all know that we are born with nothing and carry nothing when we die and yet we get involved in all sorts of money-making activities during our life. Simple commonsense tells us that needs are related to one's status and responsibilities; the needs of governors are much more than that of workers. Our greed and expectations appear to have no end and we do not know where to stop. The comments of *Bhashyakars*[2] are worth introspection; our needs

1. A learned priest in charge of temples. 2. Commentator on scripture.

are much lesser than what we imagine.

My father was a Sanskrit scholar and he knew English. He initiated Satyanandji to our scriptures and taught him Sanskrit. He used to tell me a lot about him in my childhood. I was one of those fortunate persons who saw Satyanandji. He was thinly built and had a very sensitive mind. He had come to India for leprosy mission, could not tolerate the heat of plains and was compelled to go to the hills. He was not happy with his inability to continue with the mission. He wanted to do something for the poor people. *Devbhoomi* gave him a new direction and he decided to treat these hills as his *Karmabhoomi.*[1]"

My talks with the *Purohit* continued on the next day. He told me many things about our religion. He told me that *Karma*[2] are effective till the last moment of life. He convinced me that the *Karma* of previous births have their effect on this birth but to a great extent they can be redeemed by good deeds in this very birth.

Rati during day hours kept herself occupied in social work addressing herself to the needy and doing nurse's work in the small dispensary at Thanedar. She used to get time to herself only in the evenings. I asked her about apple plantation and the development work which she had wanted to do.

"Apples," she said, "are as old as mankind. Bible mentions the story of Adam and Eve, and the apple responsible for the beginning of human beings. That besides, a few could imagine that apple would provide livelihood to the multitudes of people. Apple is a cold climate fruit and the crops are good when the rains and snowfalls are heavy. When Samuel Stokes was sent to Kotgarh church for recuperation, it must have occurred to him that this place was ideal for apple plantation. He was not the first to plant apples. Before him, Captain R.C. Scot of the British army had planted Lippin varieties of apples in Manali in 1870 but they were not liked by the Indians due to sour taste.

1. Area of activity.
2. Actions as enumerated in Gita.

The credit goes to Samuel Stokes for planting sweet varieties of apples. His efforts were so successful that these varieties have spread to all parts of Himachal. Before the introduction of apples, the farmers were getting meagre livelihood by growing potatoes and plums."

I asked her, "You had some project in your mind to improve the lot of small farmers and labour class. Have you started working on it?"

"Not yet," she said. "I am still at the learning stage. It would take time, I have been here only for one year but I am at it. As it is, there are many organisations and associations including a department in the state government which are working on research and development, and improvements in various fields to make apple growing more lucrative. Apple is the main crop in the state and these organisations are concentrating their effort on increasing productivity and profit margin. They are working in easily accessible areas. As for me, I am going to concentrate on small farmers and labour working in the remote and difficult regions. You have seen them climbing the mountains with baskets strapped behind their backs. Their life is not easy and they do not get commensurate remuneration.

I have discussed their case with many organisations, influential people, concerned ministries and political leaders. They agree with my contention but they don't do anything. Their earnings and wages are left to the market forces.

I get foxed with this term, market forces. It is a compound and complex term which includes many agencies such as growers, labour, transporters, wholesellers, retailers, consumers and so on. The wages that these poor people get depends on good or bad crop. Import of apples from foreign countries has started in a big way and we have to compete with them for price and quality.

There are critics who maintain that considerable improvement has taken place but it is negated by growth in population. They are right in a sense that apples have brought prosperity to the state, but here in the higher reaches of hills and bitter cold, it has not made much difference. Their condition is not very different from the times of Satyanandji. My aim is to improve their lot.

Satyanandji was touched by amiable nature and simplicity of *paharis*[1]. They are poor but by no means a miserable lot. They don't indulge in violence and destructive activities. Their folklore of dances, songs and festivities are enchanting. They bear no hatred towards the outsiders and are willing to assimilate. Despite hardships, they bear a smile on their face. I feel completely at home with them."

I asked Rati if she had plans to get married.

She smiled. "I am not anti-marriage but I must find a spouse who has similar views. Husband and wife can be a tremendous source of strength to each other. Satyanandji's wife, Agnes, was active partner in furtherance of his efforts. When he was jailed and sent to a prison in Lahore, she supervised the work of plantation at Barobagh and continued with the work that he had started."

"What if you don't come across such a person?"

"Then I will go alone."

"Have you decided to spend rest of your life in Thanedar?"

"Yes."

We were back in Pune. My friends, the old timers were keen to know about my trip to Himachal. I was fully equipped and told them about the efforts and achievements of Satyanand Stokes. They did not know his name and were amazed to hear about his contribution to the progress of our country.

I knew that they would ask me about the Heart-Throb. I told them about Rati; she had decided to follow the path of Satyanand and was dedicating her life to the cause of the poor.

One of them said, "That's great news. We mistook her. It is difficult to come across such girls in the present days."

1. Inhabitants of hills

I agreed and nodded my head. With a taunt I told them that I met her brother.

One friend told me, "Do you know that Madan met with a very serious car accident in America? He has suffered multiple fractures in leg, thigh and arm. I read details in the newspaper. He will take a long time to recover. It serves him right for betraying her. Would you like to inform Rati?"

"It would not serve any purpose," I said. "She has gone beyond the petty feelings of finding delight in other's grief. She is fully engrossed in a superior occupation."

An old timer remarked, "I don't think that we will live long enough to know her achievements but that girl from Himachal is great and is on the right track."

GANGADIN

Vishal Naik liked his morning walks. It gave him freshness, time to think and exercise. He never felt at ease living in the big city. He looked forward to his retirement and leisurely pace of life in some small place away from the madding crowd and now that he had got it, he felt happy.

He had started his career as an assistant city engineer in the municipal corporation and later he became chief engineer of a big real estate company. The construction work was in full swing, boosted by growing economy and craze of people to acquire property. He had made enough money for himself; it cheered him to read his bank balance, and at the same time it depressed him. His health was deteriorating; he had developed the problems of breathing, indigestion and fatigue after physical work. The medical tests were negative and he detested doctor's prescription of vitamins and tonics. He knew the cause of his disease and also its remedy. He was convinced that the pace of work and city life was giving him problems, both mental and physical. His wife Vanita too was not keeping well and preferred to move out to some small place in green surroundings.

The concrete structures multiplying rapidly in the cosmopolitan city had pained him. Irrespective of architectural design, they appeared an eyesore to him. The high-rise buildings were replacing nature's simplicity, balance and drainage. As an engineer, he knew that all these artefacts ultimately spelt disaster for mankind. They caused floods and water logging. There was little that he could do to check the march of civilization. He did what was possible for him to do and that was to get away from the crowd. He mused himself in the thought; the world is grounded on earth, the function of the world is to create and the function of the earth is to absorb.

He purchased two acres of land 20 kms away from the city. The place was neither a suburb nor a village but something in between, a settlement of 25 houses collectively known as Sonambare. He made a cottage with open space all around and shifted to the new dwelling soon after retirement. He got down earnestly to the occupation, which was in his mind for many years. He employed two labourers and started the work earnestly on the garden. After a year's hard work, Shanti Kunj[1] acquired a reasonable shape and became a good enough place to live. What he lacked was a good *mali*[2], which the habitat did not have.

Vishal, when he was working in the city, had acquired a three bed room flat. He had lost interest in that flat but it was useful. His son, daughter in law and their two children continued to stay there, well tuned to the city life. In the beginning, Saurav did not like the idea of his parents shifting to a rural area living alone, without friends, doctors and basic amenities. However, the old man was stubborn and he did what he wanted to. His son had to go off and on to Ṣonambare to meet his parents as a part of filial duty. As the time passed and the cottage acquired a face-lift, he started liking the place. 20 kms is not a long distance and Saurav, his wife and children enjoyed going there, treating it as a holiday resort.

Saurav and his family had gone to Sonambare for a long weekend. They decided to go on an outing the next day. His father recommended picnic spots on the bank of river Taragini.

1. Abode of peace.
2. Gardener.

They selected a grassy patch. The car was parked on the road side. Saurav and Surabhi took out *duree*[1] and the basket of tiffin. Sarita jumped out with a ball in her hand and the old man followed with toddler Mukesh in his arms. Vanita was not keeping well and stayed in the house.

The day was bright and the sun was pleasant in the month of February. Saurav and Surabhi played ball with Sarita, while Vishal walked around with Mukesh showing him birds, flowers and trees. Suddenly they heard a loud humming noise of bees. They laid themselves flat on the ground covering their face. Sarita crawled inside the rug and Vishal covered the toddler inside the coat. The swarm swept past them. They heaved a sigh of relief but that was temporary. After proceeding 300 yards, the swarm turned about and once again swooped upon them. The picnickers repeated the drill to save them from the menace.

A man in his late twenties was riding a bicycle on the road. He saw the plight of the family with bees hovering around and decided to help them. He got down from the cycle, walked to a nearby place and whistled a tune. The bees gave up Vishal's family and rushed towards the intruder. They covered his face, head and the body, and remained glued to it. The man signalled to the distressed family to go away. They scurried to the car, leaving behind the rug and tiffin, and closed the doors. When Saurav started the engine, his father told him to stop.

"We cannot leave that man at the mercy of bees."

"What do you want me to do?"

"Let's give him a shelter in the car."

Saurav stopped the car ten yards short of the bee-covered man. The old man opened the glass window half way and told him to get inside the dickey.

"I am fine. The bees are not hurting me. You go away."

"How can we leave you like this? God knows when the bees will quit you."

"That's not difficult." The man whistled another tune. It

1. Rug.

was harsh and jarring. The bees started leaving him and the swarm headed towards another direction.

Vishal got out of the car and thanked the man for coming to their rescue. The man lifted the rug, basket and other belongings of the family and put them in the dickey. He picked up the ball and gave it to Sarita. Saurav opened his purse and offered money. He did not accept it. Vishal said, "We are so grateful to you. At least give us the pleasure of meeting and knowing you; you must come to our place, we live in Shanti Kunj." The man said that he had some work in hand. He promised to meet them in the evening.

"What's your name?"

"Gangadin."

Sarita had recovered from the shock and cheer had come back to her face. She waved her hand and said, "Bye, bye and thank you uncle."

Gangadin reached Shanti Kunj in the evening at the appointed time. He was treated like a dignitary and various kinds of eats and dainties were served to him. He did not touch any, however out of civility he accepted a glass of milk.

"You saved our life," said Surabhi. "I wonder what would have happened to us if you had not reached in the nick of time."

"Nothing whatsoever, that is provided that you didn't harm them. The bees after some time would have gone by themselves. I presume that someone must have disturbed them."

"That may be so but we were in a terrible situation."

"I saw that and that's why I came to your help," Gangadin said with a smile.

"Where do you stay?" Vishal asked.

"In the city with my friend."

"How do you spend your time there?"

"I am looking for a job."

"What kind of work you do?"

"I am a gardener, a *mali* by profession."

Vishal had found what he was looking for. Gangadin accepted his offer for the job. He was a very different kind of *mali*. He did not bargain for his pay and emoluments and left it to the discretion of his employer. He declined to live inside the cottage with Vishal and preferred to make a hut for himself. His carriage, conduct and speech were like a well-bred, educated person. Vishal registered that this *mali* would need a different kind of treatment.

Gangadin surveyed the area from different angles both from within and outside the premises. He examined soil and watering arrangement, and took into account sunshine and wind direction. He charted the garden plan on a big sheet of paper and discussed it with his employer.

Vishal liked the plan; it was grandiose but he was getting concerned about the expenditure part. Gangadin told him that it would not be much. For the first few months, he will have to employ some more hands for digging and preparing the soil but thereafter the existing two labourers would suffice. Good seeds and saplings are important and expensive but he would use his own. Compost would be made in the garden. The venture would start paying back after two years and it would become profitable after three years. Over the years, Vishal had been taking interest in gardening; he knew the names of flowers, seasons of sowing etc. He had read a number of books and journals on gardening and was proud of his knowledge, but here before this expert he found himself a novice. Tacitly he accepted whatever Gangadin said.

The work started in a week's time. In patches the compound was dug up and stones, pebbles and weeds were removed. Four large pits were made for compost and a nursery came into existence. Drains were made for watering various sections.

Saurav and his family had gone to Sonambare in the month of June. They were astonished to see the pace of work in the garden. The first spell of rains had moistened the earth. Gangadin asked his employers to plant a few inaugural shrubs, saplings and trees; Sarita was most delighted, she planted maximum numbers.

In a year's time, the garden in Shanti Kunj had taken shape. The seasonal flowers were in bloom, the shrubs had reached waist high and the trees were firming up. The lawns were green though not fully spread and the creepers, which Gangadin had planted around the cottage and his own hut, were growing up.

Sarita liked the garden. She insisted that she must go to Sonambare on all weekends and whenever the schools were closed. Saurav and Surabhi grumbled for the simple reason that schools have far too many holidays and it would be tiring for them to go up and down. But the little one had her way; "An hour's drive is not much of strain," she said. Vishal and Vanita were happy; it gave them opportunity to be with their grand children as frequently as possible.

Sarita and Gangadin had developed fondness for each other. Sarita liked him from the day he saved them from the storm of bees. She liked butterflies, she wanted to catch them but they would fly away. Gangadin showed her the way. He rubbed the back of his hand with exotic petals and stretched his arm. The butterflies came rushing and rested on his hand. Sarita tried the trick and it worked. She carried the butterflies on the back of her hand and showed it to her parents and grandparents. When they came near, the butterflies flew away. Sarita had a hearty laugh, "You don't know the trick."

She learnt how to call birds, squirrels and rabbits. They were at ease with her, thronged around and followed her. Gangadin had cautioned her not to catch them; just play and enjoy nature's bounty.

At the back of the cottage, Gangadin had planted certain plants. They were not decorative and there was nothing exotic about them but they had immense value for health care. Gangadin recommended leaves, seeds and extracts to Vishal and his wife. The old couple were rejuvenated. They gave up all allopathic medicines.

The second year of the garden was rewarding. Besides seasonal flowers, the shrubs and creepers had started blooming. The trees had grown beyond the height of man and the lawns flourished like a thick carpet.

Sarita had inborn talent for drawing and painting. She drew flowers, trees, brooks, mountains, sunrise, sunset etc. She showed them to Gangadin.

"How do you like them?"

"They are good."

"Tell me, how can I improve upon them?"

"Look, I am not a painter! How can I comment? All that I can say with certainty is that they are really good, very good for girls of your age."

"Ganga *Chacha*[1], you live with trees, flowers, birds and nature and therefore you are the best judge. You can tell me where I have gone wrong."

Gangadin started taking interest in her drawings. He pointed out wherever she had made mistakes in shape, size and colours. As the months passed Sarita gained proficiency.

Vishal and Vanita had developed a new zest for life. Gangadin had done a marvel on their health. They felt restless for passing on the benefit they had gained to others in the city. Saurav and Surabhi found their visit to Sonambare as refreshing. It was all due to Gangadin.

The father and son were discussing the ways and means to popularise flowers and gardens in the city. People liked flowers but they did not grow them. They came forth with all kinds of reasons such as living in flats, lack of time, absence of good nurseries, lack of *malis*, exorbitant expenditure etc. Vishal said that all these excuses were lame; basically they lacked will. What they need is a strong desire, direction and motivation. Saurav commented that people preferred to buy a slab of ice cream instead of spending money on flowerpots.

Vishal knew the mayor of the city. He invited him and a

1. Uncle.

few councillors to Shanti Kunj. They were thrilled to see his garden. They requested Gangadin to visit the city and redo the public gardens, which were in a pathetic state. The mayor said that the people must develop aesthetic sense.

The commercial growers and owners of nursery took maximum advantage. They got seeds and saplings at lowest price and doubled their income. The flower vendors became a happy lot. They procured decorative pots and planted flowers in them. The demand was rising and their business started growing rapidly.

Saurav, Surabhi and their children were going to a party. They stopped at the roadside florist's shop. They bought a good looking bouquet for the host. They were amused to read the placard— 'Gangadin Enterprise.' Sarita giggled, "We bought our own flowers!"

The third year was fulfilment of Gangadin's dream. The sustained hard work of the previous two years had borne fruit. The city held flower shows in four different gardens. A new direction was floated and the people had started taking interest in growing flowers. The roads were beautified with shrubs on either side and in the centre-divide. While driving on the roads one could see flowerpots and creepers hanging down from the balconies of multi-storied buildings. Media gave a wide publicity and TV showed clips and documentaries on horticulture. The mayor and Gangadin were praised for their efforts to beautify the city.

The press reporters and journalists visited Shanti Kunj. Gangadin kept himself aloof, however his reticence was taken care of by praises from Vishal and Saurav. Vanita told reporters about an idyllic life free from ailments.

Once Sarita asked *Chacha,*

"How does one call bees to the face?"

"Why do you want to know that?"

"Because you called them and you were least perturbed. I also want to do that."

"It takes time to learn that, besides it can be very dangerous. In any case you are too young."

"OK, but teach me when I grow up."

Gangadin felt that his task has been accomplished. Towards the end of his third year, he told Vishal that soon he would be leaving. The two labourers have become proficient *malis* and they can look after his garden.

Vishal was taken aback. He told his son about Gangadin's decision of leaving Sonambare. We need him, we cannot manage without him, and somehow we must prevent his going.

Saurav told his father that we possibly cannot withhold him. He came on his own will and now if he wants to go, who can stop him?

Vishal said, "We can give him more money and a proper house to live in. But little that I know about him, he is least interested in money and comforts. It looks that we have not been able to meet his requirements. What does he need from us? You must find that out. It may well be that someone amongst us has hurt his feelings."

Vanita said that she treated him with maximum respect but even then if some lapse had occurred, she would render an apology. Sarita said, "I will find out from Ganga *Chacha*. He cannot go."

Saurav smiled.

Vishal did not like it. "Look my son, if Gangadin goes Shanti Kunj will lose its charm. The gentry from the city will no more visit us. We have acquired name in horticulture because of him. The nurseries and plant sellers will curse us. And who will supervise parks and gardens in the city?"

"Obviously this responsibility will fall on your shoulders. You claimed to be a great garden enthusiast and an expert. Surely, you must have learnt a great deal in the last three years!"

"Well, I have been watching him with keen interest. I also took active part but I tell you I am nowhere before him. He has inborn talent and green fingers. I now realise that gardening needs expertise and knowledge as much as any other profession like engineering and medicine."

"But tell me my dear father, how did you take it for granted that he will spend his entire life here, with us?"

"I suppose that was my mistake."

"Then face it," said Saurav with mocking smile.

Vishal was fuming. It was a serious situation for him, as a matter of fact for everyone except Saurav. He said in an angry tone, "You seem to be least bothered. To me it appears that you are quite happy."

"Yes, I am."

"That's strange. You have no sympathy for him. Have you ever considered what will he do? Where will he go?"

"He will go to the place from where he came."

There was silence in the room. No one liked the attitude of Saurav, his way of talking and indifferent reaction to Gangadin's departure.

Sarita was annoyed. She yelled, "Papa, how can you be so wicked? How can you neglect my *chacha?*"

After a while, Saurav told them that he understood their feelings but they did not know anything about the *mali* that they had employed. They would change their views when they heard his story.

"Let's hear his story," said Vishal.

Gangadin comes from an established and well to do family of landlords. His grandfather had earned the title of Rai Bahadur during the British Raj. He has three brothers and two sisters. His eldest brother looks after farming and two shops. The other two brothers are doctor and engineer, well settled in the town and the sisters are married in good families. After doing high school, Gangadin opted for college education in agriculture. His eldest brother liked the idea; he wanted someone to assist him in farming. He was sent to the city.

He returned to Rambagh after getting the degree in agriculture. However, the expectations of his brothers were belied; he did not take any interest in farming. He wanted two acres of land for horticulture. The eldest brother told him that growing flowers is OK but in that small town there are no buyers. It cannot be done on a commercial basis. He could grow flowers in the house as a hobby but he must devote his time to cultivation of crops.

Gangadin was not happy. He did not visit the farm; instead he used to remain in the house reading books on horticulture. His brothers did not like his glum face and ridiculed his ideas. They nagged him for his lethargy and not paying attention to the land. It was only his mother, who had sympathy for her youngest son.

The elders in the house thought that his attitude may change after marriage. He was married to a sweet and homely girl from the same town. But that did not bring about any change in his demeanour and behaviour; he remained where he was in the state of melancholy. A year later, he was blessed with a daughter. As time passed, he became more and more gloomy and depressed. His mother was most worried. She asked, "What's wrong with you? Are you keeping good health?"

He told her that he was keeping good heath and was perfectly happy with his wife and child. His problem essentially was that of denial of what he wants to do. He agreed with his brothers that horticulture was not advisable in that small town but he could try elsewhere. It was his ambition and life's challenge. He was not asking for money or any other help. All that he wanted was to test his ability.

His mother asked him if he had consulted his wife. He told her that he has done that. The kind of venture, which he wanted to undertake, needs three years. But three years are nothing compared to a satisfying life lying ahead. He told his mother that his wife was agreeable.

"What will you do if you do not succeed?"

Gangadin said that he would come back. "I know the challenges before me. When I go to the city I will be a stranger. No one would trust me. The landlords there would be reluctant to give me two acres of land, which I need for trial. But let me try. I must make an attempt. If I fail I will be back in six month's time. And when that happens I will take wholehearted interest in farming, which is much easier than horticulture."

The mother talked to her three elder boys about Gangadin's wishes. She told them that there is nothing wrong if *Chutku*[1] wants to try out his ideas. You must understand that he is made differently. From the childhood he was fond of flowers, birds and animals. He likes them and they like him, even the dreaded bees are friendly to him. The bees don't bite him and they allow him to take out honey. Do you know why? They know who their friend is and who will grow flowers for them. There is something peculiar about him, he is made that way and we must not come in his way. The eldest brother said that he was not against Chutku. All that he wants to say is that Chutku is not mature enough; he does not know the ways of the world. Why does he want to waste his three years? He is unnecessarily trying to be obstinate.

"That's the trait left behind by Rai Bahadur," his mother quipped.

"The chances of his success are most doubtful."

"What if he succeeds?"

"It would be a triumph for him and all of us."

Gangadin went to the city and met some of his college friends. He contacted proprietors of the gardens and owners of big bunglows with large compound. The response was negative. He borrowed a cycle from his friend and started searching suburbs for a suitable area. His encounter with us when the bees were harassing us was a coincidence.

---

1. A pet name for the youngest.

In the room everyone was spellbound by Gangadin's story and there was complete silence. Vishal asked, "How did you get all this information?"

"The hurried manner of his employment had put doubts in my mind. There should be no doubt that he was good and sincere. But, if he was so good, why did he accept the job with us for nothing? I became apprehensive. What if he has some ulterior motives? I decided to find out. Once when he was away, I entered his hut and saw some letters. Unethical it would appear but I read them. I noted down his home address and made a trip to Rambagh. Thereafter I made several trips. I have told his family members about the great work being done by Gangadin and his success story. They were very happy. I want to tell you that they are good and cultured people; his mother is a venerable lady."

Surabhi exclaimed, "You did all this without my knowledge!"

Saurav smiled. "The detective in me told me to keep it as secret."

Sarita asked, "What is the name of Chacha's daughter?"

"Kusum."

Saurav said, "Gangadin has not seen his wife and daughter for the last three years. Don't you think that he should go? But we are not going to be the losers. What we have gained is friendship with a great horticulturist. He will keep on visiting us. And from next time onwards, he won't come here as our employee. He is going to stay in the cottage as one of us."

"He will stay in my room," said Sarita. She got up and started dancing, clapping her hands.

Saurav said, "That is all about Gangadin. He does not know that I have been visiting his people. I will request all of you to keep this part to yourself and not disclose it to him. We will give him a surprise when he leaves us."

On the day of his departure, Gangadin went to Shanti Kunj to say goodbye. He was meticulously dressed and looked different from his previous appearances.

Vishal said, "We will be very sorry to lose you but I suppose you have your own reasons."

Gangadin replied, "That's right. I have some pressing reasons to go, but my work is not yet complete. The city must continue its effort on beautification. I will have to make a few more trips. I came here for certain reasons and I am glad that it has been accomplished."

Vanita offered him a glass of milk. Surabhi showed him sweets and this time to her surprise he took a piece from all dishes.

Vishal gave him four envelopes. They contained currency notes, "These are your earnings."

"I don't need money," Gangadin said. He took only ₹ 500. "This would be sufficient for my ticket and travelling expenses."

Saurav said, "Your ticket to Rambagh has been purchased and the berth has been reserved."

Gangadin was puzzled. How did Saurav know about his native place? He was more puzzled when Sarita gave him four books of her drawings. "These are for Kusum."

Gangadin was bewildered. "It looks that you have found out about my antecedents!"

Vishal told Gangadin that Saurav had been going to Rambagh and informing his family about his achievements. "All is well in your family and they are eagerly waiting for your return."

It was time for Gangadin to leave. Vishal's family came out of the cottage to say good bye. Saurav was going to drop him at the railway station. When they were leaving, Sarita said, "Ganga *Chacha,* when you come next time, teach my papa how to call bees to his face."

"Why that?"

"For doing detective's work, secretly."

SUKANYA

Bidki[1] was thoroughly confused. She could not answer any question asked by the interrogators. She did not know the name of the village, address of the house, name of her parents, relatives etc. She was victim of an earthquake in Latur, the sole survivor of a family at the age of three.

Latur is a south-eastern district of Maharashtra bordering with Karnataka and Andhra Pradesh. On 30 September 1993, the place was rocked by earthquake at 0356 hour when the people were sleeping. There was no warning of the disaster and utter confusion prevailed. The intraplate earthquake was not very severe; it measured only 6.4 on the Richter scale but the focus was shallow in depth. The shock waves caused maximum damage due to faulty construction of houses and huts. Latur is situated on Balaghat plateau approximately 600 metres above sea level. The area had been free from earthquakes for many decades and the entire zone was considered as safe. The practice in that area was to make walls with stones and join them with mud plaster. Stone plates were used for roofing and strong foundation was not considered necessary.

The stones were locally available in abundance and the

1. Small girl.

cost of construction was cheap. When the earthquake occurred, the foundation became loose, the walls gave way and the roof collapsed killing all those who were inside. The casualty figures were very high; about 8000 people had died and more than 30000 were wounded. The earthquake had mainly affected Latur and Osmanabad districts though the tremors were felt in a wider area. A large number of villages were completely destroyed.

Dinu Phadke was the headmaster of Government High School at Walmiki Nagar in Latur. He had gone to Tuljapur to offer prayers at the temple of Tulja-Bhawani. The moment he learnt about the disaster, he rushed back to Latur. Luckily for him his house, wife, children and the school buildings were safe. He got down to relief work immediately.

He was given the task to accommodate 1500 victims of the earthquake. The school was closed; the class room furniture was removed and dumped into one corner, the rooms were emptied and ad hoc arrangements were made for kitchen and toilets. By 3 P.M. the displaced people had started arriving. They were coming empty handed with no beddings, clothes or cooking utensils.

The district administration was gearing up for aid and rehabilitation of the victims. By evening, the first batch of aid workers and medical teams from the nearby towns had arrived. The government of Maharashtra had activated its disaster management scheme and help was sought from the army. Many social and philanthropic organisations came forward to provide food, clothing, shelter and medical aid. Latur was working day and night to retrieve from the grim situation.

The first task was to extricate people from the debris of collapsed houses. In Latur district alone, 37 villages were completely destroyed, 3670 people were killed and 446 were seriously injured.

On the following day, when the headmaster and his wife had

gone to supervise the arrangements in the school, he noticed a small girl in a torn frock being questioned by the aid workers. The interrogators wanted to establish her identity but she could not give them any information. All that she was saying was, "*Aai kuthe and baba kuthe.*[1]" The moment Dinu Phadke saw her, he felt that he knew her. He asked his wife, "Isn't she Sukanya?" His wife nodded. He called aloud—Sukanya. There was no response. His wife shouted—Bidki. The girl immediately looked behind at them but did not recognise them. "Of course she is Sukanya," said Parvati. She scrambled to her house, located within the premises of the school, and brought an album of photographs. She showed a photograph to the girl, the little one immediately recognised her parents and cried '*aai, baba.*[2]'

The girl asked, "Where are my *aai* and *baba*?"

"They have gone to the temple of Bhawani."

"When will they come?"

"Soon, when their work is over."

Parvati went to the rehabilitation office. She told them that she was taking the girl to her house. She had to fill certain forms and sign in the register. It became obvious to Phadkes that Sukanya had become an orphan, but she was not destitute. She came from a well to do farmer's family.

The work for rehabilitation was going on in full swing. The relief camps were being established to provide shelter, food, water and other necessities to the affected people. The injured were admitted into hospitals for treatment. The state government started an elaborate scheme for construction of houses, payment of compensation and help in resettlement of the people. Inherent in such activities is the problem of identification and legitimacy of the claimants.

Ten days had passed. Parvati told her husband to go to the

1. Where is mother? and Where is father?
2. Mother, father.

municipal office and file Sukanya's claim to the land and property. It involved three houses and 30 acres of agricultural land. The headmaster was well known in Latur. He met the concerned official and gave him an application regarding Sukanya's claim to the parental property. The clerk took Dinu Phadke for a cup of tea to a shop nearby and briefed him about complications in the case.

The clerk said, "Sukanya is a minor. She will have to establish her claim in the court of law. Her name obviously does not figure in the land records. I want to tell you that there are two other claimants to the property. One is some Shri Kolte; he claims to be the brother of Sukanya's mother and the nearest relative of the deceased family. There is another person called Dighe Patil; he claims to be a cousin of Sukanya's father. You see, a dispute has already arisen on the ownership of the property. I have never come across these two persons before. They keep on pestering me for information. Masterji, I know you; I brought you here only to forewarn you about the complications. I would advise you to engage a good lawyer to fight out the case."

On return, Dinu Phadke told his wife about the two other claimants. Parvati asked him if they knew about Sukanya being alive. "Not so far but they would know it very soon." Parvati laughed at the mockery and people's greed for property and said, "They would get a shock when they learn about Sukanya being alive, it would serve them right." The headmaster was cool; he told her that Sukanya's claim might run into rough weather and we might have to fight out her case in the court of law. He told her to preserve photographs, letters and other documentary evidence in a safe place.

The two claimants detested each other and did not see the face of the other. They had aspired to be the sole inheritors of their deceased cousin, Bhikaji Patil's property. Independently, they used to visit *Talathi's*[1] office and ascertain latest development. They were bewildered when they learnt that Sukanya was alive. From where did she come on to the surface? *Mamaji*[2] and *Chachaji*[3] had avoided meeting each other so far, but in view of the new development they decided to meet as soon as possible. They expressed grief at the loss of their cousin Bhikaji and other members of the family.

"Do you know that Sukanya is alive?"

"Yes, I heard that from the clerk."

They decided to meet Sukanya next day in the evening. They planned to meet at the tea shop and thereafter go together to the headmaster's house. They spent the rest of the day with their *Vakils*[4] to work out their future course of action.

Next day when they met, Mamaji said, "It looks that we have lost our case. Sukanya would inherit the property of her father."

"Yes, but she is a minor. She will have to prove her legitimacy and one of us will have to accept guardianship and responsibility for her upbringing."

"I have a doubt. Is she really Sukanya? How did she survive when everyone else was crushed under the roof? I do not know if some clever person is tutoring that girl to grab the property."

"You have a point," said Chachaji, "but I would not be able to recognise her. Last time when I saw her she was six months old and since then she must have changed her looks."

"That should not be a problem. I and my wife had gone to Shellary only three months ago and we had stayed there for good fifteen days. I won't make a mistake."

"That's good. We would know that very soon. We would be able to find out if some dirty trick is being played. You know how it is when it comes to property. People can go to any length."

1. Tehsildar.
2. Maternal uncle.
3. Paternal uncle.
4. Lawyer.

"If she is not Sukanya, we will have to fight a very long battle in the court of law. It would be very expensive but the property is worth a fortune and is worth fighting. We cannot let it go to a crooked third person."

"That's right. We can join our resources together and share expenses. We can reap the benefits later."

"My problem is that I live in Nanded and it would not be possible for me to visit Latur frequently. As it is I have stayed here for a fortnight which has posed many problems to me."

"I live nearby. I would be able to take care of local requirements."

They shook their hands in friendship and some kind of agreement.

Mama and Chachaji reached the house of Dinu Phadke. They were welcomed by the headmaster.

"I am so happy that you have come. We were getting worried about Sukanya's future."

The two relatives expressed shock on the tragic death of Bhikaji Patil and other members of the family. They said that fortunately Sukanya was alive and they volunteered to look after her. Sukanya was brought in. Mamaji called her near with affection and said, "Do you remember me?" Sukanya did not recognise him and did not go to him. Parvati said that the little girl was in a state of shock. All that she repeats is *aai* and *baba*. After sometime, Parvati and Dinu went inside into the kitchen to fetch tea and eats for the visitors. Sukanya went out to play. The visitors were left alone. They talked to each other in whispers.

Chachaji said, "You were right in your suspicion, she did not recognise you and so she isn't Sukanya. Someone is playing dirty trick on us and we must find that out."

Mamaji replied, "No, she is Sukanya. But wait, the game is not yet over; we can make use of the fact that she did not recognised me. We will talk later."

Dinu and Parvati returned to the hall with trays of tea and eats. They sat down around the table and talked about the calamity faced by the people and their ill fate.

The call bell buzzed. Two relief aid workers brought in a wounded man with his arm and thigh in plaster. They lowered him on to *divan*[1]. It was a surprise for everyone. The wounded man was no other than Bhikaji.

Mama and Chachaji were quick to respond. They touched his feet in obeisance and thanked God for the mercy. Bhikaji was feeling pain due to jerks in the journey; he felt better after sometime. Delighted Sukanya sat near the pillow and gently stroked his head. Dinu Phadke and Parvati heaved a sigh of relief.

Bhikaji narrated his story. He wasn't in Shellary on the dreadful night. He had gone to his *sheti*[2]. He was sleeping under a thatched roof hut. The tremors were severe, the wall collapsed and the roof fell down. He was seriously injured. The farmhands carried him up to the main road and handed him to relief workers. He was put in an ambulance and sent to the hospital at Osmanabad as Latur hospital was fully packed. Luckily for him the hospital there had better facilities. He was operated upon and put in plaster. When he gained consciousness he was desperate to know about his family. He could not move out and requested aid workers to give him the information. The news that he got was shocking; they told him that his village had been completely destroyed. The news on TV and papers was dreadful. He had to stay for a fortnight in the hospital and when he was discharged he came straight to Masterji's house.

Mama and Chachaji did not stay for long. They departed saying good-bye to Masterji and wishing a speedy recovery to Bhikaji. When they went out, their faces were sullen and they did not shake hands or bid farewell to each other.

---

1. Settee.
2. Field.

Phadkes were happy that their friend had returned and the little girl's future was safe. They were wondering as to how many innocent people would get involved in such fake claims and the outcome.

As the time passed, Bhikaji was feeling better. He sent a message to the farmhands and the labour force that he was alive and would be visiting Shellary as soon as possible. He hired a small flat nearby and shifted there with his daughter. When he visited Shellary, he was shocked by the sight of total devastation. Living there were his parents and two younger brothers with their families. The three houses were next to each other sharing common walls. Seven adults and ten children, which included his two sons, had died in one stroke. And that was the plight not only for him but hundreds of others who lived in the village.

The plaster was removed after six months. It took him one year to get back to normal life. He bought a motor cycle and made trips to his land from Latur. Meanwhile Sukanya got used to the new pattern of life. She became very friendly with Masterji's children, Anuj and Arundhati. She spent the day time with them while her father was at work.

The civil administration had completed the immediate tasks of retrieval, medical help and monetary assistance to the victims. The tented camps were ready and the school buildings were vacated. They were now engaged in long term plans. Specific funds were earmarked by the state government, and help was sought from the World Bank and other philanthropic organisations. Work was undertaken for reconstruction of 37 villages which were completely destroyed. In Latur city, new colonies were planned for the victims. Bhikaji applied for a three bed room dwelling.

A year later, Bhikaji married a girl called Niyoshi. He was hesitant; the age difference was excessive, he was forty and she was only twenty-five. Dinu Phadke had advised him to get married as early as possible; it would do good to his daughter and in his situation the children were desirable. Around the same time, the new house was ready and they moved into it. The house was located in a posh area with all modern amenities like shopping complex, banks, hospital and a school. His farm was doing well; Latur is famous for the quality of pulses, the yield was good and he was getting good money.

The time passed happily and everything looked good. Niyoshi was blessed with two sons—Manoj and Manish. As the boys were growing up, Bhikaji noticed change in the behaviour of his wife. Sukanya was getting neglected.

He confided his problem to Dinu and Parvati. "How do I explain my relationship with Sukanya? We are the survivors of the greatest disaster that can ever occur in a family. I love Sukanya and that is something which my wife does not like. Well, I am equally fond of my sons but she does not think it so. Now, how do I convince her? She is not prepared to listen to me. I had visualised this problem and it is getting from bad to worse."

Dinu and Parvati saw the point. Step motherly treatment is a known phenomenon but they thought that Niyoshi would show better sense. She came from a poor family and ought to be grateful to God for what he had given her.

Dinu said, "I feel most awkward because I had advised you to get married. I did not realise that it will take such an ugly turn. But, what are you going to do now?"

"I am thinking of putting her in the hostel. She is now eleven years old; children at that age are sensitive and I do not want her to suffer from any kind of depression."

"Not a bad idea," said Parvati. "It may do good to both—Sukanya and Niyoshi."

Bhikaji with his daughter had gone for a stroll to a park. Tactfully he opened the topic; he was overwhelmed by her reaction. She said, "Baba, you and I are survivors of tragedy.

We know how difficult the life can be. I won't find any difficulty in living in the hostel, but tell me— will you come to meet me sometimes?" They hugged each other. Bhikaji said, "I will and that too very frequently. I want you to know that you are my most precious possession."

Sukanya was sent to a local hostel near the residence of Masterji. She was happy to be close to her friends—Anuj and Arundhati. She was good in studies and responsible in her behaviour. Latur is well known in Maharashtra for the quality of education. She came in the merit list in high school examination and took admission in the college for graduation.

Niyoshi felt happy. She was left free with her sons. Manoj and Manish had started going to the school. They were being pampered and this was not to the liking of Bhikaji. Whenever he tried to correct his sons, Niyoshi flared up. The boys understood that their father was inconsequential. He told his wife that farming needs hard work and the boys should be trained for that. Niyoshi dismissed him by saying that she would do that at the appropriate time.

Fifteen years after the earthquake, Latur had made tremendous progress; it was no longer one of the backward region of Maharashtra. The government had made a comprehensive project document 'The Vision 2030' and steps were being taken to achieve targets set therein. It covered various aspects on education, agriculture, irrigation, industries, information technology, infrastructure and so forth. The communications were improved and the city was well connected to Mumbai and Hyderabad by road and rail. Regular flights were introduced between Mumbai and Latur. Many survivors of the earthquake had become rich and Bhikaji was one of them. His land had become very productive, as good as any, in other parts of the country.

Sukanya did graduation and thereafter she appeared in the

combined civil services examination. She informed her father and Masterji about her success in the examination. She sought their blessings for the interview.

Dinu Phadke asked, "Which service are you going to join?"

"Police," she replied promptly.

"Good," said Parvati. "We need women in that force to clean up the society."

In the ordinary course Bhikaji would never have permitted that, but knowing the situation in the house he did not say anything.

Manoj and Manish were growing up; they were in class XII and X. Niyoshi ignored the advice of her husband and continued to pamper them. They were getting any and everything that they wanted—food, clothes and pocket money. They had become lazy and indolent and had put on weight. Manoj had failed in the examination. Bhikaji was convinced that Manish would do no better.

Bhikaji had gone old. At the age of sixty, he did not have strength and energy to visit his farm daily. He shifted to his village leaving his wife and sons behind at Latur. He felt more peaceful in living alone.

Niyoshi was beginning to realise her mistake in the upbringing of children. The boys scolded her and did what they liked. They spent most of their time with friends and never missed a movie. Somehow, she still felt that better sense would prevail on her sons and they would become responsible.

Sukanya joined Sardar Vallabh Bhai Patel National Police Academy, at Hyderabad. She had grown into a smart, tall and tough looking girl. She passed out amongst the top ten and got her choice of Maharashtra cadre. She applied for posting to Latur on compassionate ground and that too was done. She was given charge of a subdivision.

Bhikaji and Phadkes were very happy. Sukanya liked Latur because of her friends. Anuj had taken up a job in a bank and

Arundhati was teaching in the degree college. The two families got together on a Sunday; Niyoshi had come and she talked for a long time with her step daughter. Sukanya bore no ill feelings and Niyoshi respected her. She knew that she will have to rely very heavily on her daughter in the coming years. What she did not know was that her daughter asked for posting to Latur just for that reason.

Manoj and Manish had become incorrigible. They could not pass secondary school examination and after three attempts they were expelled from the school. They had started drinking and Niyoshi suspected that they might be consuming drugs. They were always in want of money and when they did not get that, they stole jewellery, trinkets and silver from the house. Niyoshi had now realised her mistake and frequently recalled what her husband had said. Her only hope was her daughter; the two brothers were scared of their sister.

The affluent Latur was showing typical signs of big cities. The hotels, restaurants, clubs and bars had multiplied manifold. Parties, late nights and eating outside had become a fashion. Drinking beer during day and whisky in the evenings had become a norm for those who could afford it. The girls were becoming promiscuous with their hairstyle, makeup and revealing dresses; saris were on their way out. The orthodox, the middle class and the older generation did not like this part of change.

But, there were other things which were of greater cause for concern. The crime rate had gone up. Drunken driving, juvenile delinquency, illicit distillation, and drug trafficking had set in. Large number of visitors coming from big cities wanted a good time and the call girls were in demand. The girls working in bars and restaurants attracted attention. Theft and robbery had become a common occurrence. Sukanya in the course of her duty was getting acquainted with these problems; these were part of her responsibility and she was thinking of ways and means to overcome them.

Niyoshi was terribly upset. Manoj and Manish had gone out on the previous evening and did not return. She tried to contact Sukanya but the latter was not available. Finally when she got her, she told her daughter about their absence. Sukanya told her mother to wait. She contacted the police stations and got the information. Manoj and Manish had got involved in a brawl at Centurion Inn hotel. They had committed theft of the hand bags of two foreign ladies and were found in a drunken state. The security staff of the hotel informed police and they were taken into custody. The medical examination revealed that they had consumed alcohol and found a trace of drugs.

"Can't you use your influence to get them released?"

"Ma, I can try but how would that help? Our concern should be that they should get over the menace of alcoholism and drug addiction otherwise such incidents will recur. This has to be done before it gets too late and they fall victim to AIDS."

"What should we do for that?"

"We have to rehabilitate them. Unfortunately good de-addiction facilities are not available in Latur. They will have to go to Mumbai. If that is done the punishment will get mitigated and I may be able to help."

"How much time will that take?"

"Three to six months but I want to warn you that relapse can always take place. When they return, they must not stay in Latur; they know the contacts here and can easily fall a prey. They should go to our village and stay there because the drugs are not likely to be available in that place. They would be able to get over this menace if we exercise caution for the next two to three years. Ma, I must tell you the reasons why they fell to this abuse. It was due to the lack of harmony in the house, absence of discipline, easy money and too much of freedom. I am sending you some books; please go through them, they would be eye opener."

Niyoshi read the books. She consulted a few doctors and friends and realised the grim consequences of alcoholism and drug addiction. She was convinced that she would have to take lead in rehabilitating her sons. She told Sukanya to go ahead with her plan. The boys were sent to Mumbai.

Sometime later when they met, Niyoshi said, "When the boys return, I too am going to the village and join my husband."

"That's good. For total cure they would need a happy family life, the discipline of joint family, caring for each other, group activity and physical occupation."

"I will leave the keys with you. Would you be able to look after this house?"

"That won't be a problem."

Several women's welfare organisations had met Sukanya on her posting to Latur. They were proud of having a lady police officer in the city and wanted to make best use of her. They complained to her regarding all kinds of crimes being committed on women; the worst of which was *vyasan*[1]. The main sufferers were poor women in slums and notorious villages. She listened to them patiently and promised to give all possible help.

Sukanya recalled the discussion they had on the subject in the police academy. The problem was continuing from the earliest times and the ill effects were well known. Consumption of alcohol was permitted by most of the state governments and those who imposed prohibition were not very successful. Where did police come in? Their job was to prevent illicit distillation and sale.

Brewing country liquor has a long history. It is made in all parts of the country from local produce such as grains, fruits and flowers; the most commonly used base is sugarcane. The process is simple; cane juice is poured in to a large cauldron, certain chemicals are added and the juice is allowed to ferment. After fermentation, the closed cauldron is heated for which cane bagasse is used as fuel. The vapours pass through a coiled tube, which is cooled by water, to get alcohol. Cost wise it is very cheap; the equipment is simple, no tax is involved and

---

1. Addiction.

overhead expenses are nominal. The *bhattis*[1] are easily made in the fields and their numbers are so many that the police cannot keep a track on them. Destruction of bhattis does not make much of a difference; the others come up in no time.

Sukanya was gathering information. Vaghoba in Latur was a known don of this trade. He supplied equipment to the brewers, tested the product and bought the produce. He was clever; he employed reliable agents, kept various activities in separate compartments with no knowledge about others and kept himself aloof. He was convicted for this offence before but after release, he reverted back to the old trade as a more cautious and clever person. Instead of destroying *bhattis,* Sukanya was concentrating her mind to catch this gangster.

The maid servant of the police officer had ushered in a middle aged woman from the village of Konda. It was nearing office time and Sukanya took her to the office to hear her grievances.

The woman said that her village is going to face a serious law and order problem relating to illicit distillation.

"What's that?" enquired Sukanya.

"Godaru is a man who advances money for distillation and buys the liquor. This time a dispute is going to take place as the farmers want more price for the sugar cane."

"Do you know Godaru? Can you recognise him?"

"Yes I had seen him a few years back. His face is peculiar because of very broad temple, sunken eyes and short ears. He cannot be mistaken."

The face that the woman had described was akin to that of Vaghoba. The police officer was getting interested. From the criminal's dossier, she pulled out a photograph and showed it to her. "Is this man Godaru?"

"Yes."

"Are you sure?"

"Absolutely. I told you that he cannot be mistaken because of his peculiar features."

---

1. Furnace.

"Does he visit your village every year at the beginning of brewing season?"

"No."

"Then how do you know that he is going to visit this time?"

"He has to. He fears that if he pays more money to our farmers, he will have to do the same at other places. That he does not want to do."

"Look, it is a case of price negotiation. Where do I come in? No crime has been committed. It is for you people to sort out your problems."

The woman pleaded, "The crime will be committed. I know it for certain. The farmers are adamant, Godaru is not going to give in and scuffle is going to take place."

"From where did you get all this information?"

"My husband told me. She hesitated for some time and said, "He is a brewer; our livelihood depends on that. He has been trying for settlement but has not been successful. They want to have direct talks."

"Did your husband tell you to meet me?"

"No. I came on my own. I fear that my husband's life is in danger."

"When is the meeting going to take place?"

"The date has not been decided so far. I will inform you when it is fixed. It would take place in the open area next to Bhatti late in the night."

Sukanya analysed the information. Godaru was no other than Vaghoba whom she wanted to apprehend. The woman appeared to be sincere and the dispute was realistic. Her problem was— will Vaghoba go to that place himself or depute someone else? She decided to organise a raid. In plain clothes she went to reconnoitre the village of Konda. She identified *bhatti* and open area next to it. The area was surrounded on all sides by sugarcane crop. She made out a plan and kept it to herself.

On the evening of the raid, a truck was hired and she got into it along with ten armed constables. Tarpaulin was lowered to hide the police force. The truck reached Konda by 8.30 P.M. in the night and the force dismounted. The driver was told to proceed another 5 kms and wait for call for the return journey. Sukanya briefed the force regarding their task. They walked to the open space and hid themselves in the sugar cane field.

Sukanya had detailed a reliable head constable to keep an eye on Vaghoba. He kept watch on the house and around 6 P.M. reported that ten ruffians had entered the house and amongst them two were armed with guns. That was the time for her to start. An hour later he reported that two jeeps had entered the house. Around 9 P.M. he reported that the jeeps loaded with men had left the house. The head constable on motor cycle kept a track on the movement of jeeps. At 10.30, he reported that the jeeps were 15 kms short of Konda. He was told that his task was over and he could go back.

The police officer and her party heard the sound of footsteps. The two parties, one of the farmers and the other of the don, sat down facing each other in the light of hurricane lamps. Vaghoba was telling the farmers that if the price of sugarcane is increased, the cost of liquor will go up and he would lose the business in the competitive market. The farmers were saying that farm inputs had become expensive and it was for Vaghoba to cut down his huge profit margin.

The arguments were heating up. Vaghoba would not budge and the farmers would not yield. One of them said, "We have found another party to give us better price," and asked Vaghoba to leave the place. This infuriated Vaghoba. "How dare you say that? I have been paying you wretched people for the last five years." He took out his pistol and fired a shot on the farmer.

Sukanya and a constable had crawled forward from the hiding place. They were just ten metres away watching them and listening to their conversation. In the heat of their arguments, the two parties did not notice their presence. When the shot was fired, Sukanya took out her revolver and fired at

Vaghoba injuring him. The constable blew the whistle and the police surrounded them flashing their torches. The two parties were completely taken by surprise. Vaghoba and the ruffians were apprehended.

The local newspapers praised the police officer for her daring feat and bold action. The parents and Phadkes felt proud of her. But the bureaucracy followed its own way. She was transferred to Aurangabad.

The women's welfare organisations were agitated. They felt that the posting was prompted by the nexus between the politicians and the underworld. Sukanya was at pains to convince them that she had completed her tenure; she possibly could not stay in Latur for the rest of her service.

Bhikaji decided to have a get together before her daughter moved out. The venue was fixed at Shellary, his ancestral place where the new house had come up.

The farewell party was becoming emotional. Bhikaji said that Sukanya had saved the family from ruination. Niyoshi confessed her mistake and expressed her gratefulness. The brothers promised that they would keep away from drugs and alcohol. Dinu Phadke and Parvati said that it was a chance event that they had spotted her. Already she has done a great good to Latur; it remains to be seen what all she does in future.

Sukanya was feeling awkward with such praises; she went to the adjoining room with her friends, Anuj and Arundhati.

Arundhati asked, "Where and when do we meet next?"

"In Aurangabad, sometime in February."

"That is after two months. We can't wait that long."

"You must give me time to settle down in the new job."

There was something which the police officer did not tell her friends. She had learnt from the headquarters that she was recommended for Police Medal to be announced on the Republic Day. She wanted to meet her family and friends after the presentation of award.

I WANT TO PLAY

Latif and Hamid were studying medicine in Chicago.They became friends because of their similar views on life and pursuit of ideals. Latif belonged to Hyderabad and Hamid hailed from Karachi. They were liberal and modern in outlook, free from the shackles of religion.

After their graduation they returned to their countries and started practising medicine. They remained in contact and visited each other off and on. Besides friendship, there was yet another reason and a very valid one; Latif's wife was from Karachi and Hamid had married a girl from Hyderabad. When people said that it was Allah's blessing, they laughed it off; for them it was just a case of coincidence and nothing else.

Latif was late in returning to his home. It was a hot day and the traffic jams were irritating. His eyes were aching due to the glare of headlights.

"You are late, what happened?"

"Oh, the rush of patients and the mad traffic."

He changed his clothes and eased himself in the rocking chair. The air conditioner was a great relief and a cup of tea cheered him.

"Mariam, there is a good and bad news."

"What's that?"

"Hamid, his wife and daughter are coming shortly?"

"That's good. What's bad news?"

"He has developed a cardiac problem."

Hamid deliberated the problems associated with his ailment and his wife's desire to go to Hyderabad. The operation could be performed in Karachi but that would delay his wife's going; it could also be done in India. There was no dearth of competent doctors in that country and besides being cheap the hospitality services were good. The operation would involve two months of stay and that would give plenty of time to Jahanara to stay with her parents. At seventy, her father was a sports enthusiast; Jahanara had not visited him for the last two years and he was missing her and his granddaughter.

For the last one year, Hamid had been working very hard to complete his book 'Facts and Myths.' That was in pursuance of his ideals to educate people on the advent of science and technology and thereby help them to get rid of religious dogma and anachronous practices. The book was in three parts: Part 1 contained essays on the origin of cosmos, descent of man and gradual development of mankind to the present stage: Part 2 contained the various benefits given to the mankind by sciences and technology and Part 3 contained instances of myths and blind practices, which people follow to this date and must get rid of. He visited several publishing houses and was pained to get their negative response. His last visit was to Millennium Publishers; he met a very modern and polished editor but here too he failed.

"Mr Hamid, I have gone through the manuscript. It is very well written and frankly I have liked it but I am sorry we cannot publish it."

"Why?"

"Your book will invite criticism from the religious leaders and we may be threatened by the terrorists."

"But that is precisely what we must fight!"

The editor smiled and shook his head.

Hamid was keen to get his book published at an early date. However, something else had occurred which was of immediate concern to him. He felt discomfort in the chest and went for a cardiac check up. The angiography revealed a major block in the main branch of left coronary artery. Surgery was a must and earlier the better. He rang up his friend Latif to ascertain if he knew a good surgeon in Hyderabad. Latif told him that a very renowned doctor, Prabhakar Rao worked in the same hospital and advised him to take the earliest flight and reach Hyderabad.

At the airport, Hamid's condition was checked in the ambulance. His blood pressure, pulse and temperature were within normal limits. He was taken straight to Shahnawaz hospital and lodged in a comfortable room. Next day angiography was carried out once again and tests were carried out to meet pre-anaesthetic requirements.

In the evening Dr. Prabhakar Rao came to visit Hamid. He told him that the operation would take place on the next day. He was particularly nice to Jahanara, "I don't see any problem. Your husband will be alright after the operation. It would do you good if you offer prayers to God."

The surgery was carried out at the appointed time. It lasted for four hours. He was then taken to the intensive care unit where he stayed for the night. His condition was stable and next morning, he was shifted to the private suite. Latif was with him during the night; he had passed urine and did not suffer from any side effects.

Dr. Prabhakar Rao did not come to see him for the next two days. Latif told Jahanara that Dr. Rao was a very busy person but that did not mean negligence; he kept track of his patients.

In the evening when Dr. Rao came, he asked the patient, "Do you have any complaint?"

Hamid said no.

He told Latif that his friend was OK and fit for discharge. He should bring him for check up after a week. Latif said that he would obtain discharge papers, settle the bills and take away the patient on the next morning.

"Rubbish," exclaimed Dr. Rao. "Take him now; he will feel more comfortable in the house." He asked Jahanara if she had performed prayers. She nodded her head. "That's good," he said, "I would like to spend some time on worship but I don't get it. I feel happy when others pray; it helps me indirectly."

Dr. Rao's eye fell on the manuscript lying on the table. The title 'Facts and Myth' aroused his curiosity.

"What are these papers about?"

"A book written by my friend," said Latif.

"The subject is interesting; may I glance through it?"

"Sure."

Dr. Rao went through the contents and turned the pages in a hurried manner. He expressed desire to go through the book. "I won't take more than a week."

Hamid was taken to Latif's place; that was done because of doctor in the house. He went for walks in the morning and evening and the distance increased gradually. After a week he went for check up. Dr. Rao declared him fit. Hamid had a question to ask-

"Was my condition due to sedentary work, long hours of writing, lack of exercise and sleep?"

Dr. Rao laughed. "The facts are that you got heart attack and the reasons are like myths. That reminds me, I scanned through your book; it is good. My younger brother, Manohar was thrilled by your writing. He is a writer, he wants to meet you."

"That would be my pleasure," said Hamid.

After a week, Hamid joined his wife and daughter in the house of his father in-law. Jahanara's father was a wealthy businessman. He owned a palatial house with a tennis court, a swimming pool and a cricket pitch. Sports were his hobby and passion.

Latif and Mariam had come to meet their friends.

Mariam said, "Almost a fortnight has slipped and I had no time to talk to your daughter. Where is she?"

"Must be playing or watching TV. Let me call her."

Zahira was a well built and tall girl. She was twelve but looked more than her age. Her arms and legs were long and muscular like an athlete.

"What were you doing?"

"I was watching TV. Yousuf Pathan is about to complete a century."

Mariam said, "You are coming to us this evening for dinner. What would you like to eat?"

"Anything."

"That part is OK but what is your favourite?"

"I like to play," said Zahira and ran away to watch Yousuf Pathan.

Jahanara said that the girl was incorrigible. She was spending all her time in playing games; she appeared to have inherited the traits of her grandfather.

Zahira was happy in her grandfather's house. She had company of six boys and girls and all of them played games. She had developed fondness for tennis; she was a beginner and no match to her cousins but she was determined to reach their standard. When her cousins went to school she played alone with the help of ball boys. She also practised on the wall. In fifteen days she had made considerable progress and was able to join her cousins in the game.

The old man used to sit out in the mornings and evenings to watch his grandchildren at play. He was amazed to note the progress made by Zahira. Once when she was practising on the wall, he drew a circle and asked her if she could repeatedly hit the ball inside the circle. She could get it 6 to 7 times out of 10. That was remarkable.

Zahira had picked up the game well after a month's hard

work; she could play with the boys, her serves and shots had equal power.

One day grandpa asked her—

"Have you heard the name of Sania Mirza?"

"Yes, I have seen her play on TV."

"Do you want to meet her?"

"Yes," she said with a smile.

Manohar Rao was happy to meet Hamid. He was a man of letters, well known in Osmania University. He himself was a writer and knew local publishers. He complimented Hamid for his work.

"The best thing about your book is the style of narration. The facts are known but they have not been assimilated by the people. It is not that they do not know what science and technology has done for them, they watch TV and see the development that has taken place in the western countries and yet they are hesitant and don't take a bold step forward. They follow old ideas and customs, which they should discard. I suppose that's the message you want to send across."

Hamid nodded.

"It is a good book by all standards. Have you sent it for publication?"

Hamid told him about his bitter experience and negative response from the publishers in Karachi.

"That should not make any difference. You can get it published here."

"I don't want to do that. You can call me rigid and obstinate; I insist that the book must be published in Pakistan."

"God only knows when they would be bold enough to do that. Meanwhile you are denying the benefit to the readers. It equally applies to other religions as it advocates scientific temper."

"I am primarily concerned with Muslims. They are misusing religion. The call for jihad, violence and terrorism are not in keeping with the spirit of Islam. Pakistan has gone on a wrong track and that is why I want this book to be published there."

"You have a point; you are the author and therefore the choice is yours, but there are ways and ways."

A fortnight's regulated life of diet, walks and rest had improved Hamid's health considerably. In the evenings he could sit out, chitchat with his friend and occasionally enjoy a drink.

"What's the situation like in Pakistan?"

"Democracy is back struggling for survival. The roots are flimsy, not firm and one does not know when the tree will fall down."

"You mean that there is a possibility for the army to get back into power?"

"That threat has always been there and will continue. The military have dug in well and cannot be dispensed with. They are a power by themselves and do not submit to civil control. I do not know why our generals have taken upon themselves the responsibility for governance."

"That's because they do not have any work. I am glad that the Taliban are keeping them employed."

They had a hearty laugh.

"What's progress on the Taliban front?"

"Military action is going on but to tell you the truth we are in a confused state. The politicians, the military and the religious leaders have their own vested interest and they want to profit by the presence of Taliban. The fact is that Pakistan had given shelter to Osama Bin Laden and his followers. They promoted terrorism and Taliban movement. Now that the attempts are being made to throw them out, naturally they are retaliating. Over the years they have been able to make strongholds, store destructive material and consolidate backing of fanatics. "

"Does it mean that the Taliban will also continue like the military?"

"That is how it is and will continue for many years. America and the whole world is exerting pressure against terrorism. Much will depend upon the people of Pakistan. It is they who have to realize that they live in a globalised world, which respects everyone's faith and civil rights. Osama has been taking the advantage of 14th century Islamic scholar who divided the world into two groups i.e. 'the house of Islam' and 'the house of non-believers' and thereby justified jihad and terrorism. These leaders have taken full advantage of criminal elements in Muslim society. They want to create an environment in which the Muslims must feel that they are a community apart who cannot live with others. They want to wage war between Muslims and non- Muslims and in that process they have harmed millions of innocent Muslims who are looked upon as suspects. If we want to live peacefully in this world we have to change our beliefs and attitudes. I do not know what Osama is up to; he has threatened the whole world—US, Western countries, India, Israel and so on. This is being stupid. Such actions would threaten the very existence of Islam!"

Hamid had become emotional and Latif felt that his friend had done enough of talking for the evening. He kept quiet.

Hamid was recovering well. The two friends met almost every evening. They never had so much time with each other ever since their college days. Hamid said, "Thank God I decided to get the operation done here."

"I recommended it to you because Dr. Prabhakar Rao is really good and has a tremendous reputation. It was convenient and cost wise very cheap."

"Jahanara and Zahira are happy and it has given me the opportunity to be with you. To tell you frankly, I have not been able to make friends in Karachi. I do not know why?"

Latif smiled. "It is not easy to make friends. Tell me, did Manohar Rao meet you?"

"He did. He was interested in early publication of the book. He said that if there are any difficulties in Pakistan, it can be published in Hyderabad."

"Not a bad idea."

"But I don't want to do that. Why can't my views be published in Pakistan?"

"You know the reason; in the present environment the publishers will play safe and therefore it will take a long time."

"Manohar Rao had suggested an alternative. Vernacular versions in Hindi and Urdu can be published in India."

Latif thought for a while. He advised his friend to agree to the proposal. A book to spread scientific temper is a universal requirement applicable to all religions. He reminded his friend that the number of Muslims in India is more than that of Pakistan.

Hamid saw the point and gave his consent.

The grandfather took young Zahira to meet Sania. He knew that family well. He used to admire Sania's father for his efforts to encourage and coach her. Right now he was doing the same thing for his granddaughter.

Imran Mirza took a liking for Zahira. He watched her play during the next few days and was impressed by her. He told Mushtaq Ahmed that his granddaughter had a great potential.

Zahira was taken to the doctor of sports speciality. Her heart, lungs, limbs and various joints were examined in detail and she was declared fit.

Imran advised Zahira to play in his court with better players. One day she was thrilled when Sania entered the court and played with her for 15 minutes.

Mushtaq asked, "What do you think of my granddaughter?"

"She is a prodigy. This year she should play for sub juniors and next year she can take part in the juniors. I have a feeling that she would be able to play for the open when she is sixteen. I must confess that she is better than what Sania was at her age. She is going to be a tall girl, taller than Sania and that means more power and reach."

"Tell me if she should take on tennis as a career?"

"In my opinion she must."

The two friends were going through the newspapers. Bomb explosions had become a common occurrence in Iraq, Afghanistan and Pakistan. Hamid was perturbed by the latest explosion in Karachi; it was close to his house. He exclaimed, "What kind of nonsense is this? Normal life is becoming difficult in Pakistan."

Latif nodded. "It looks to me that Karachi is not a safe place. It may not be advisable for you to go back."

Hamid smiled. "You know, this very morning my father in-law was telling me that Zahira has taken a liking for Hyderabad and that is because of tennis; Jahanara was born in this place. He was throwing a hint if I would like to settle down here."

"Not a bad idea. I also feel that way. You have no close relatives in Pakistan and it would make me happy."

"Come, come. I am not going to get scared by the terrorists. I am sure that Pakistan will pull through. I was born there. I am proud of my country and I want to do my bit for its reformation. There is something on which I seek your views. Where did Pakistan go wrong? I am asking you because what is happening today must have a cause for the beginning."

"Pakistan was created on the basis of religion, but instead of using religion for promotion of faith, brotherhood and universal peace, it was exploited for personal gains. The referendum conducted by Zia-ul-Haq was a sham. He became the President alright but placed the country under terrible religious influence. When the political leaders take shelter behind religion, it is the religious leaders who start gaining upper hand and very soon the fanatics and fundamentalists assume control. They unleash a reign of terror and enforce their code of conduct. In India we have had this experience but luckily it did not last long."

Hamid said, "You are right. The worst part of the religious movement is that the genuine religious teachers who believe in God are pushed to the back seat. The fanatics have not only assumed control but have turned the country into a centre for international terrorism. This is obviously wrong. A time will come when people all over in the world would speak one language, lead similar life style and the religions would lose much of their proscribing power. We have to move in that direction. Unfortunately the religion is coming in the way and obstructing progress."

Latif said, "That's right. I will go a step further. The world is open before us; we can pick and choose and select the best. The religions want us to live in a closed cordon, like frogs in the well. We must learn to put religion in its place, retaining good points and discarding the rest. There is no harm if religions learn from each other."

During dinner Mushtaq proudly used to announce progress being made by Zahira. "This girl will bring a great name to our family. Her ground shots are good; she has to improve serves and volleys and that will take place in due course. Her game at the age of 12 is commendable."

It pleased Jahanara to hear good words about her daughter but there was something, which was troubling her mind for the past few days. She told Mariam, "All this is OK but she will have a tough time in Karachi."

"Why?"

"She is playing here in blouse and shorts and that will not be permitted in Pakistan."

Mariam saw the point as she knew the situation in Karachi. "Have you told this to your husband?"

"No. I don't want to open serious talks with him in his present condition. He is terribly emotional and keeps on ruminating on the same point. I am quite convinced that he got heart attack because of his worrying nature.

You see, as it is, we are not liked by the orthodox elements. Zahira is obstinate and she will insist on playing in shorts and that will create rancour. You know Mariam, there are many people in Karachi who do not practise Islam; they go to night clubs, drink and dance but they are sensible. They do it discreetly. And here is my husband who takes pride in violating tenets of Islam. He is vocal, there is no requirement for it and now he wants to publish a book.

I do not know why is he doing all this? I am not well read like him but common sense tells me that all religions are man-made, full of myths. They will disappear with the spread of knowledge and until then we must show patience."

"I see your point," said Mariam. "We are a denied lot but we have patience more than men. I will tell my husband to counsel Hamid. He does not believe in outdated practices but he is sober and not a rebel."

During the night chat, before going to sleep, Mariam told her husband about Jahanara's problem. She told him that you people talk so much about social and global issues but here is something of immediate concern within the family and that needs to be sorted out. Latif promised her to do the needful.

Hamids had gone to Latifs for dinner.

"What's the latest?"

"Manohar rang up. He asked me if I would like to read the translated version of the book. I told him that my knowledge of Urdu is not good and Hindi I do not know. I have left it to him."

"You did a right thing. You can trust him; he is thorough and sincere."

Hamid said, "You have been asking me a whole lot of questions on Pakistan. Tell me, what is happening in India?"

"The democracy has taken a firm root; the general feeling is buoyant, full of hope. We have a whole lot of problems pertaining to religions, castes, backward classes, tribes and regional differences. The open society, despite diversities, is doing well. All sectors are progressive and the economy is sound."

"What about Muslims?"

"I knew that you would ask me this question. Well, the Muslims have natural religious affinity with people in Pakistan and like us they have relatives and friends in either country. But that apart, people watch on TV the happenings in Iraq, Iran, Afghanistan and Pakistan. They certainly don't want Taliban.

The leaders in Pakistan can make statements which can please only Pakistanis but they appear utter lies to us. How can we tolerate their terrorist activities on our soil? The worst and the most shameless attack was on Mumbai.

The Muslims in India are late starters but the awakening is taking place. A considerable change in outlook has taken place in the last 20 years. They want development. They are taking on to modern education and are freeing themselves from religious dogma. Muslim girls are coming forward and joining the work force. But the backward pull exists; what can one say if a prominent religious leader ridicules Shabana Azmi as *Nachane gane wali ladki.*[1]"

Hamid asked, "Do you think that Indo-Pak relations will normalize?"

"They should but I don't see possibility in the near future. The politicians, the military and the religious leaders have been taking full advantage of anti-India posture. It will take time for the people to wash off feelings of hatred which has been ingrained in their minds."

A brief spell of rains had cooled the weather. The evening was pleasant. Latif asked his friend if he would like to have a drink. He nodded.

Latif had to resolve the problem being faced by Jahanara. Hamid appeared to be relaxed. The time was opportune to open the topic.

"You would be going back to Karachi in two weeks. Dr. Prabhakar Rao told me that you can resume your work."

"Yup, I have rested for a long time and now I am getting

1. The girl who sings and dances.

bored. I must get back to my work."

"Jahanara was saying that Zahira has picked up tennis well and she has a great potential."

"That is quite likely. She is very fond of games and least interested in studies."

"She will miss tennis in Karachi. Over there, she would not be allowed to play in scanty dress to which she has got used to."

"She can switch on to other games."

"What if she insists on playing tennis?"

"I haven't thought of that. I am sure she would understand the constraints in Karachi."

"I am not so sure," said Latif. "She may decide to choose tennis as her career."

"That is what my father in-law wants her to do; he is a dreamer. To pursue sports as a career is difficult. I am not against it. I would obviously like my daughter to excel in sports but it is not easy; very few can reach that level."

Latif smiled. "Let me correct you. Mushtaq Ahmed is not a dreamer. He is a very practical person and has been at it very systematically. He has been obtaining expert opinion on her potential and has got her medically examined. Zahira is lucky. She has got a place here to stay and Karachi is not far away. You can always meet each other a few times in a year."

"It is more of Jahanara's problem. She would find it difficult to live without her and therefore let her sort it out."

Mushtaq Ahmed's views were simple and straight. A good sportsman is simply born; it has nothing to do with parentage, religion, race or country. But if grooming is not done the talent gets wasted, uncared for, like gems in the caves of ocean. William sisters became great because they were born in America; Sania reached her spot because she was born in India and was coached. It should be a social responsibility to discover talents at an early age and give them direction.

Zahira had shown talent, resolve and tenacity. Mushtaq

wanted his granddaughter to rise higher than Sania and be amongst the top ten of the world. He was going to do just that. One morning he asked Zahira,

"Do you want to pursue tennis as a career?"

"Yes."

"For that you will have to stay here. Would you do that?"

"I will ask my Mom."

Hamids were getting ready to go back. Jahanara was spending time to buy essential household requirements which were not easily available in Karachi. She asked Zahira if she wanted anything; she did not show any interest.

Only two days were left for them to go. Mushtaq's entire family had assembled for the gala dinner.

Mushtaq told Hamid and Jahanara, "You have to take a decision; if you want your daughter to become world class tennis player she will have to stay here and train herself."

Jahanara asked, "Can't she switch over to another game?"

"What rubbish are you talking about? Every game has different requirements and she is made for tennis."

Jahanara realised her mistake and kept quiet.

"Look, I understand your feelings but you have to make some sacrifice in the interest of your daughter. It won't take long. In four years when she is sixteen we will know where she stands. If she is not up to the mark, I would myself advise you to take her."

Hamid said, "We can do that but it would be better to ask Zahira what she wants."

Zahira was upstairs with her cousins. She was called and asked the question. Three times she said 'I want to play' and ran back.

GODAVARI

The thirty odd travellers were suddenly and collectively gripped by fear. Their bus had stopped at an isolated spot, about 10 kms ahead of *Sfatic Shila*[1], on a gravel road from Chitrakoot to Gupta Godavari. A log was lying across the road and that was a bad omen. The driver had no other option but to stop. The area was known for dacoits who robbed passengers and took away their belongings. Silence fell on their lips and they did not know what to do. The driver of the bus and the conductor told the passengers to get down quickly and remove the log, hoping for the best.

The passengers had barely got down. They were traumatised by sound of horses approaching them. Four dacoits with guns in their hands were charging towards them. The travellers were huddled together; two dacoits dismounted from their horses and collected the booty of cash, watches and jewellery. They were then told to remove the log and proceed ahead with their journey. But that was not all. The gangsters asked four young girls to stay behind. The driver and the conductor were told to pick them up on the return journey from that very spot. The fear stricken, servile passengers had started boarding the bus; just then a female voice, clad in nine yards *dhoti*[2], roared- "Stop this nonsense!" The four young girls yelled,

1. Marble rocks.
2. Sari.

"We will not tolerate this!" The shout of the girls made an impact on the travellers. A male voice burst out, crying "*Jai Durge.*[1]" It was followed by others shouting, "*Har Har Mahadev.*[2]"

The horses were first to react. Not accustomed to such shrieking noise, they started bucking and rearing. The dacoits got involved in controlling their horses; that was the first thing for them to do. The two dacoits who had dismounted from their horses to collect loot were finding it difficult to get back on the horses. This encouraged the people. They brandished sticks and shovels. Some amongst them picked up stones and pelted them at the animals. The horse of the gang leader turned about and bolted in the reverse direction. The other three followed suit. In that flutter, the bags containing the coveted booty dropped from their hands.

The log was removed and the bus was ready for onward journey. Some of the passengers were keen to take their belongings. The leader girl said, "Not here, you can take them leisurely in the bus." The bus resumed its journey.

Chitrakoot is a well- known place for pilgrimage. Ram, Sita and Laxman spent eleven years of their exile in this place. From Chitrakoot, private buses take the pilgrims to Sfatic Shila, the *Ashram*[3] of Anusuya and Gupta Godavari. Sfatic Shila is the first spot. Here, the River Mandakini is at its best with blue waters skirting around marble rocks, against the backdrop of *Arjun*[4] trees. Sita loved to bathe here and do her *shringar*[5]. Ram, seated at a distance, admired her beauty and form, while Laxman kept vigil. A crow, enticed by the beauty of Sita, constantly gazed at her and would not fly away. This annoyed Ram; he fired an arrow blinding the crow.

The ashram of Anusuya is the next spot. It lies in the thick

1. Invocation to Durga.
2. Invocation to Shiv.
3. Hermitage.
4. A species of tree.
5. Make-up, adornment.

of the forest and is the source of River Mandakini. The devotees have built a temple in her remembrance. The place is serene; ideal for meditation and to this date remains an isolated spot unspoiled by civilisation.

Gupta Godavari is the final place. Legend says that the River Godavari from down South wanted to meet Ganga. She moved along subterranean passage, but from here she could not proceed further and became *gupta.*[1] Throughout the year, the cave remains flooded and springs keep sprouting up, but the water does not go anywhere else. This part puzzles the pilgrims.

The remaining part of the to and fro journey was pleasant for the pilgrims. There was no hold up anywhere. They sang *bhajans*[2] to pass time. Two of the girls were good singers and gave them lead. After the incident, the travellers had developed respect for the girls and fellow feeling amongst themselves. During the journey, they looked sideways and behind to get the glimpse of the girls and at halts they tried to make acquaintance. Their focus was on the leader girl in dhoti. Her name was Godavari.

Godavari and four girls were doing teacher's training at Crosthwaite College in Allahabad. The girls had decided to visit Chitrakoot during the holidays. This incident made them intimate.

Kalavati asked Godavari, "How come you showed such courage?"

"I was reminded of Ahilya."

"Ahilya was victim of Indra's lust and treachery. What has that to do with this incident?"

"It wasn't that Ahilya who was turned into stone by the curse of Gautam rishi and later revived by Shri Ram. I was inspired by another Ahilya, Ahilyabai Holkar of Indore. In 1754, her husband Khande Rao died and she became a widow at a young age. Her son, Mal Rao was a minor and she became trustee of the kingdom. A few years later, Mal Rao died and the kingdom

---

1. Vanish, disappear.
2. Devotional song.

was left without a male heir. Raghunath Rao, Peshwe of Pune, made a claim on the kingdom to spread his empire and if necessary threatened to take it by force. Ahilya stood by her right and resisted any such move. She raised and trained an army of women. She sent bangles to Raghunath Rao and challenged him to the battlefield.

The battle did not take place. The Maratha Sardars advised Raghunath Rao regarding the absurdity of his venture and declined to fight women's army. Raghunath Rao had to reconcile with a glum face."

"It is a curse to be born as female. Men take advantage of our weakness and exploit us as much as they can," complained Gayatri.

"That happens because we submit," said Godavari.

The girls talked about their plight in the society. Godavari agreed with all that they said, but ended up by saying that some of us have to devote our life for emancipation of our sex.

Godavari was born in Hoshingabad in Madhya Pradesh. Her father was a petty construction contractor with uncertain income. He lacked business acumen and as the years passed, his inherited property was dwindling. He told his children that he was unfit for business and impressed upon them that they should never get into that profession. Vaman Rao insisted that his son and two daughters must concentrate on studies and pursue academic career. Mukund, Godavari and Gangu were aware of their pecuniary condition; they understood it well that they will have to stand on their own feet.

The boy and the two girls were brought up in a thrifty environment of low middle class, sharing household work with their mother. Out of the three, Godavari excelled in studies. Her favourite subject was Sanskrit. As a school going girl she wrote poems in Sanskrit. She had the unique privilege of reciting them before Shankaracharya in a temple gathering. The *Dharma Guru*[1]

1. Preceptor of religion.

was impressed by her and blessed her.

In 1910, Vaman Rao expired. The responsibility to run the family fell on the young shoulders of Mukund. Soon after completing B.A. he took up a job of teacher in Prayag and shifted there with his mother. Meanwhile, Godavari and Gangu had moved to Mumbai for college education.

That was the end of Bhadkamkar family's stay in Hoshingabad. In the later years, whenever they recalled their childhood, they remembered the river Narmada most. In Hoshingabad, the river is wide and deep and its water is crystal blue. The three children were good swimmers. Every morning they used to go to the *Ghat*[1] for bathing and thereafter they visited the temple built by Ahilya bai.

Pandit Madan Mohan Malviya was one of the most venerable figures of India during pre-independence days, ranking amongst great men like Ravindra Nath Tagore and Mahatma Gandhi. He was a freedom fighter and took active part in the struggle for Independence. His greatest contribution, however, was in the field of education. The British had laid the foundation of modern education by opening schools and colleges. The three Presidencies i.e. Bombay, Madras and Calcutta had universities for higher education, but there was none in the rest of the country.

Malviyaji was a staunch Hindu. He chose *Banaras*[2] as a site for his university, the seat of learning from the ancient days. He made a beginning by establishing Central Hindu College and two schools, one for the boys and the other for girls. But his mind was set on *Vishva Vidyalaya*[3]. He met Maharaja of Ram Nagar, who happily gifted him vast land at Assi and beyond. He collected funds from princely states and business community. The Banaras Hindu University came into being and teaching commenced from the year 1916. He assumed the responsibility

1. Pavement on the river bank.
2. Varanasi.
3. University.

of vice chancellorship and remained in chair till 1938.

In those days the state of education for girls in the country was appalling. Strangely, the worshippers of various Goddesses and *Shakti*[1] did not consider education as a necessary attribute for women. The awareness existed only amongst the select few of a small segment. Malviyaji was aware of this weakness in the society; the parents were hesitant to send their daughters to the schools. He made a beginning by starting a middle class school for girls in *Kammachha*[2]. The response was not encouraging and there was an urgent need for improvement in this direction.

Malviyaji had a dream of making a women's college in the university campus. The college has to get students from the schools but unfortunately the city had no high schools for girls. Most urgently, there was a need for a dynamic principal, who would change the state of affairs. The post was advertised in the newspapers.

Godavari, after completing M.A. in Sanskrit from Bombay University, was looking for a job. She applied for the post. Her interview was unique. Malviyaji had heard that name from Shankaracharya. The latter had mentioned to him about a promising girl from Hoshingabad who wrote poems in Sanskrit.

Malviyaji asked, "Have you ever met Shankaracharya?"

"Yes. I had recited my poems before him."

From that time onwards, the two of them spoke to each other in Sanskrit. For half an hour, the rest of the selection committee, not versed with the language, remained mute. Malviyaji asked her many questions about her ideals, hobbies and future plans. He was impressed by her and the appointment became a certainty. He, however, advised her to do teacher's training course before assuming charge. And thus, Godavari had landed up at Crosthwaite College, Allahabad.

The incidence at Sfatic Shila had several good and lasting after

1. Goddess of might.
2. A locality in Varanasi.

effects. Out of four, three girls—Kalavati, Gayatri and Sudha volunteered to join her at Banaras. Godavari told them that she might not be able to give them salaries commensurate with their qualification. "Never mind that," said the girls, "at least, we will lead an honourable life and do some satisfying work." Three trained teachers in a small middle school was a great asset.

The tough looking young man who had raised the cry of Jai Durge offered himself for the service.

"What will you do in a girl's school?"

"I will protect you and the girls."

Godavari needed that. She was not happy with security arrangements and Jawahar was absorbed. He remained in the school for many years till his retirement as most trusted watchman and was liked by all. The driver and the conductor of the bus too offered their services but there was no requirement.

A man in early thirties had become her most ardent admirer. During the trip, he was seated behind the girls listening to their conversation. He was working as accounts clerk in a degree college at Allahabad. He introduced himself as Suresh Asthana.

"Ours is a small school up to middle class. We cannot afford an accounts clerk; we collect fees ourselves and maintain account."

"You will need one and that too very soon."

"How do you know that?"

"I can read it from your face. Call me whenever you need me, my services would be available to you whenever you want me."

Godavari took over the charge of the school after completing teacher's training course. The school had only one building, which housed headmistress and the teachers on the ground floor and classes from 3 to 6 on the upper floor. The number of students was around 60 girls from nearby areas. The first thing that she did was to make a brick lined courtyard for morning prayers. The school session began with Vande Matram and Saraswati Vandana.

She with her three colleagues from the college at Allahabad

made an elaborate plan for the construction of full fledged girl's high school with hostel facilities, play grounds, auditorium and other requisites. The plan complete with all details was sent to the university office for approval. Three months had passed; nothing concrete had taken place and there were only queries. Godavari got fed up. She went to meet Malviyaji. She told him about her plan and frequent abortive visits by *tonga*[1] to the university office.

"Strange," said Malviyaji, "I do not know any thing about it. I presume that the office must be examining all details before putting the papers to me. Your ideas are laudable, but it requires enormous efforts for acquisition of land, construction of buildings, appointment of teachers and host of other things."

"I have done all that," said Godavari.

"That's good, but having done that, there will be a requirement of funds and that is always a major problem."

"I do not need funds." Godavari said assertively.

"How will you manage that?"

"The same way as you did. I will follow your path. *Mahajano yen gatha sa pantha*[2]."

The resolute confidence on the face of Godavari shook Malviyaji. He closed his eyes and went into contemplation. That was a practice recommended to him by Shankaracharya—concentrate your thoughts on the vexed problem, controlling all your senses, before taking important decisions. After sometime, when he opened his eyes, he said, "Go ahead, *Yashasvi Bhavah*[3]."

Diwali is festival of joy celebrated all over in India; the customs however vary from people to people and region to region. For *Marwaris*[4], it is the time to close account of the previous year and when they make profit, they spend it lavishly. Kirori Mal

1. A horse driven conveyance.
2. The path taken by great men is direction for others.
3. Blessing for success.
4. Business community.

was acknowledged as the richest grain merchant of the city. That year he had made a record profit. He called his daughter Sarla and asked her what gift would she like to have for Diwali? Sarla was indifferent, being on a different wavelength. She did not pay any attention to her father's offer. He told her that according to the custom, the money has to be spent otherwise *Lakshmi*[1] would not be happy. Sarla told him that Lakshmi would be more pleased if she goes to *Saraswati*[2].

"I don't understand you."

"Look, next year I am going to finish class 6. There is no class 7 in the school and that would be the end of my education. *Sister*[3] is planning to raise the school up to matric level, for which she needs money."

Kirori Mal was struck with what Sarla had said. This part had not occurred to him. His wife endorsed her daughter's view. The grain merchant held a meeting of all marwaris known to him and impressed upon them the dire necessity for girl's high school, run on Hindu ethos. The response was immediate and overwhelming. He collected a huge amount of donation on Deepavali eve.

Jawahar had stopped Kirori Mal outside the school gate. He had heard the name of the reputed grain merchant. He had no objection to his entry but he would not permit four burly looking men who were guarding the box containing cash. Politely he said, "We permit only parents and close relatives."

"Who will guard the cash?"

"We will do it," said Jawahar.

Kirori Mal was courteously escorted to the school office. Godavari was holding a meeting of teachers. She was telling them that the plan for the expansion of the school has been approved. Now onwards, she would be devoting most of her time on raising of funds and meeting donors. The teachers must act on their

---

1. Goddess of wealth.
2. Goddess of learning.
3. Godavari was called as sister.

own without her guidance. In the middle of the conference, she was told about the visit of the grain merchant. The meeting was put on hold and Kirori Mal was called inside.

The grain merchant told Godavari about the intent of his visit. He was taken to the prayer hall. With obeisance he placed the box in front of the marble statue of Saraswati. The box contained 2 lakhs.

That evening, Kirori Mal told his wife that our daughter was safe in that school. He was impressed by the security arrangements. The security of their daughters was a prime consideration for parents and that was one of the important reasons why they did not approve of their education.

'Aaj' and 'Sansar' were the two most popular Hindi newspapers of Banaras. They gave wide publicity to Godavari's grandiose plan for the upgradation of middle class school. It appealed to the educated community of the city. They came forward with all kinds of assistance including money.

Kalavati was incharge of collecting fees from 60 odd students and its accounting. She found herself in a terrible state handling visitors and donations. She had never seen so much of cash and was not versed with banking. An urgent letter was sent to Suresh Asthana. He came in a week's time and assumed the charge. He organised a very efficient and honest office for the school.

With monetary assistance pouring in from different quarters, Godavari earnestly got down to the expansion of the school. Land was acquired and Malviyaji laid the foundation stone of the new building. Godavari made trips to the princely states and collected more funds.

The buildings, which Godavari was constructing, were latest in design. *Aaj* and *Sansar* published monthly review on the progress of construction. Sarla and her class friend's were thrilled to see the 7th class coming into being.

While the construction work of the school and its expansion programme was in progress, Godavari received shock on her personal front placing additional burden on her shoulders. Her brother Mukund had died. She went to Prayag and brought her mother and the young widow. Indira had a four year-old daughter and was carrying a child in her womb.

The widows in those days were meted a very harsh treatment. They were required to shave their heads, not allowed to marry and were considered as sinners to spend their rest of life in the backyard. They were debarred from all social functions. Godavari prevailed upon Indira to shed old ideas and face the world squarely. She was admitted in the school and completed her education. Later she was absorbed as a teacher.

A few years later, Godavari had to confront yet another discomforting situation. Her younger sister, Gangu was not getting along well with her husband. Gangu was bold; she decided on separation and lived with her four growing up sons for their education. Her daughter Malti was sent to Banaras for school education.

Godavari was now required to run a home. There were five other members— her mother, Indira with her two daughters and Malti. Gangu and her sons went to Banaras regularly during vacations. She loved the company of children and was perfectly at ease with many people around her; she believed in more the merrier. Jawahar did shopping and Janaki, an old maid did cooking. It was an open house for every one and people were welcome at any time. She had fostered the feeling of *Atmiyata*[1] and *Apanapan*[2]. Indira was called as *Bhabhiji*[3], Jawahar as *Bhayya*[4], clerks as *Babuji*[5] and teachers as *Bahenji*[6]. For herself, she liked being called as Sister and that meant— she was approachable to

1. Fellow-feeling. Affinity.
2. A feeling of one's own kind.
3. Brother's wife.
4. Brother.
5. A respectful name for Clerks.
6. Sister.

staff and students at any time. Running the home did not in any way affect her work in the school.

By 1925, the Central Hindu Girls High School was functional. Inspired by Sister's example, qualified teachers from good families joined the faculty and quite a few came from outside. The girl's hostel had become popular under the supervision of Bhabhiji. It gave facility to outsiders for education of their daughters and that too in a place like Banaras. The girls from distant places including Nepal derived the benefit.

With the passage of time and political stir for freedom, social awareness was on the rise. People were becoming alive to the necessity for the education of girls. There was a clamour to raise additional capacity in each class. The school at Kammachha had become their favourite. The cultural activities in the school appealed to them. The parents were pleased to see their wards taking part in the plays of Kalidas, classical dances and music. The emphasis was laid on teaching of English, sciences and mathematics in Hindu environment. This made the school different from others. Here was a school run in a family atmosphere with no hierarchical distance at any level and in perfect security.

In 1930 two more buildings were constructed to accommodate growing number of students, which had crossed the figure of 600. The Montessori sections were added for the tiny tots. To cater for girls, living at a distance from Kammachha, three busses were purchased. The driver and the conductor from Chitrakoot came willingly. They brought additional hands including a mechanic.

Godavari had planted creepers along the periphery of the prayer shed. The 'Blue Bells' had grown and the foliage completely covered the sides and the roof. '*Lata Mandap*[1]' became an idyllic spot for staff and students and the prayers sung here made indelible impression on their mind.

---

1. A shady enclosure covered by creepers.

Doctor Mrs Thangama enjoyed a good reputation in the city as a physician. She took charge of medicare of staff and students. She had lost her husband a few years ago and was issueless. Once she told Godavari that she felt very lonely. Sister advised her to get married.

The doctor smiled and said in a lighter vein, "Let both of us get married. You have a better claim; you are younger, good looking and active."

Sister too smiled. "Look, I am not lonely. There are so many children in the school and my house is always full. It is you, who is facing the problem. There is nothing wrong in widows getting married."

"Tell me, have you never felt a sexual urge?"

"Of course I did when I was young. But circumstances were such that I got involved in matters of immediate concern. To begin with I had to get a job and later I got involved in family problems and development of the school. The sexual urge remained suppressed in some corner of my mind and now, it is dead."

From 1940 onwards, Godavari lived a relaxed life. She had completed her mission and not much was left for further development in the school.

Her mother had died. She was very old, past 95 years. She was bedridden and had gone senile. The old dame had a wish; she wanted to breathe her last at Kashi. Godavari was happy that her mother's wish was fulfilled.

In 1941, the Banaras Hindu University had completed 25 years of existence and a special convocation was organised to celebrate the occasion. The function was attended by Mahatma Gandhi, Dr. Rajendra Prasad, Pandit Jawahar Lal Nehru, Sardar Patel and host of other leaders. Godavari had a chance to meet the luminaries. She was most happy to meet Sarojini Naidu.

Sarojini was a poet. She was aptly called as 'Nightingale of India.' She joined the freedom movement in 1905 and had the distinction of becoming the first woman president of Indian

National Congress.

The two women had certain common features. They were of similar built and complexion. They were brilliant in studies and wrote poems. There was a glow on their face of indomitable courage, confidence and dedication. The difference was— one followed Gandhi and the other Malviya.

Sarojini was senior by more than ten years. She complimented Godavari for her efforts. She told her that the country will attain independence within a decade but progress will depend upon education.

Simplicity is a virtue, which all great men and women share. It is obvious that if one dedicates life for others, own life style must be simple with minimum requirements. For herself, Godavari followed the teachings of Upanishad— "Take that much as you need, the rest belongs to the society." Our rishis made a noteworthy comment, "Our requirements are far lesser than what we imagine."

Mahamana[1] Madan Mohan Malviya died on 12 November 1946. That was the greatest shock to Godavari and thereafter her health started deteriorating rapidly. Doctor Thangama said that Sister had developed the problem of irregular heartbeat and malfunction of kidney.

In the spring of 1947, she told Kalavati, Gayatri and Sudha about her desire to visit Ahilya Ghat. They knew that Ahilya was a role model for Godavari. Her wish was complied with. She looked cheerful and good. Sudha told her that if she showed courage, the way she did in Chitrakoot, she would conquer the ailment, but that was not to be. Godavaribai Bhadkamkar breathed her last on 12 April 1947 at the age of 55.

Godavari died at a young age but in that short span she achieved her ambition. The bus incident at Sfatic Shila had fortified her resolve to work for the emancipation of women. Once when she was in Allahabad, she read a poster— "The key to the

1. Malviyaji in his later years was called as Mahamana for his noble mind and lofty ideals.

development of our country lies in education of women." She stuck to it.

Life is governed by situations and the circumstances were not kind to her. Her brother's death at an early age and sister's separation from her husband posed additional responsibilities on her. But she went through it with a smile. Before her death, Indira and her two daughters completed their education and were settled; Gangu's daughter was married and her eldest son completed M.Sc. from Banaras Hindu University.

Godavari was fully satisfied with her achievements. There was, however, one thing which she lamented. She wanted to see the country's independence. She missed that by four months.

The Women's College in Banaras Hindu University was holding a function on Teacher's Day. The students had invited their ex-principal Sarla Gupta as guest speaker to deliver the address.

Sarla, Kirori Mal's daughter, had done her schooling in Kammachha and thereafter joined the Women's College in the university. She had done M.A. in history and taken up the job there itself as lecturer. She became principal after 30 years and had retired in 1975.

Sarla was requested to give a talk on 'The Status of Women in India and their Future.' She told the audience about the plight of women from the earliest times and their neglect in the society. And she also told them that whenever women stood up, they were successful, enjoying full support from their male counterparts. She quoted examples from extant history. She said that much remains to be done and after Independence, it ought to be our responsibility to uplift the status of women. The future will depend upon what we do. Turning to the teachers, she reminded them about their well-articulated task of building the nation.

She told the audience that the present situation has greatly improved; the women are free to pursue any career and while we enjoy the benefits, let us not forget the contribution made by our predecessors. She spoke to them about the life and deeds of Godavari, the lesser Malviya in every sense of the word.

DUKHIA

It was evening time. Akshay Pande was sipping tea in the garden of his bungalow at Lonavala. He was trying to recall the name of a Bihari peon who had retired long ago. He could recollect the face, features, accent and all other details but somehow his name was slipping. He was very fond of him and therefore the memory lapse was ridiculous. He asked his wife—

"Do you remember the name of Bihari *mali*[1] who used to look after our garden?"

"So many Biharis have worked in our garden. Which Bihari are you talking about?"

"That tall and slim fellow with a long moustache."

She recollected that mali but she too could not recall his name.

Akshay after completing his graduation in zoology and specialization in fishing technology had taken up a job in Tata Power Company as manager for Mahseer breeding, which the company had accepted as part of their corporate social responsibility. The site chosen was a rain fed lake near Walwhan Dam with a spread of 2 square kms. It was a beautiful place like a holiday resort.

1. Gardener.

Akshay liked the job; it suited his temperament and provided scope for the development of his hobby. He was a bachelor at that time and had to live in a lonely place. The Bihari was his best companion both during the office and after office hours.

Next day when Akshay went to his office, he asked his personal assistant to dig out the old dossiers of peons. "I am interested to know about a Bihari peon who had retired 15 years ago."

"What was his name?"

"Dukhia."

Akshay smiled to himself. How was it that he could not recollect the name yesterday? He had no answer for the memory lapse.

Dukhia had repeatedly requested him to visit his place in Bihar. He could not make it due to his involvement but now the opportunity had come.

It was only a week ago that he received a letter asking him to proceed to Patna. Dorabji Tata Trust, an organisation for corporate social responsibility, was doing excellent work in Bihar for fish breeding in village ponds and promoted self-help groups for women. He was called for consultation. He was wondering as to what kind of consultation was he required for? His specialisation was Mahseer and not the table fishes like Rohu, Katla and Mrigal.

In Patna, he was told that his help was required for extension of fishery scheme to interior areas bordering on tribal belt. If the scheme became successful, it could later be extended to the tribal areas. The state government was very keen to see the project through and was willing to give all possible help.

"That is OK but where do I come in?"

"We understand your point," said the General Manager of Dorabji Trust. "Your specialisation is game fish for the sport of angling and ours is that of table fish. The two fields are different but the state government is insistent on calling you and that is why you are here. The government have identified a village called Khajaria in Darbangha district. That area has a large number of ponds, gets good rains, is not densely populated and is suitable for breeding fish."

"That's good but what advice can I give you?"

"We don't need any technical advice but your presence is required for something else," said the general manager. "Let me explain. The area is relatively backward and that is because it is not connected by good road. The place continues to be dominated by the *zamindar*[1] and his gang. The *Thakur*[2] does not like encroachment by outsiders. We sent a team to examine the situation in that place. The report was negative in that the zamindar treats ponds and all the natural resources as his property coming down from generations. He is averse to formation of cooperative societies and empowerment of women. He is favourably inclined to fish breeding provided it is under his control. This condition is not acceptable to us."

Akshay smiled. "It is a case of law and order; if the government is so keen let them send a contingent of police to that place."

"We discussed this point. The government is not going to locate police and incur extra expenditure for the sake of fish breeding."

Akshay was feeling irritated. "But what do you expect from me?"

"I am coming to that. There is an old man in that village. He knows you; his name is Dukhia. He has told the minister for fisheries that you alone can solve the problem."

"Look, I know Dukhia. He was my peon in Lonavala. I am very fond of him; I still remember the way he looked after me in my bachelor days. I am indebted to him for his services and to tell you the truth; one of my reasons to come here was

---

1. Landlord.
2. Eldest member in Rajput family. Here Landlord.

to meet him. But how can I be of any help in this matter?"

"I agree with you. I had expressed similar views to the minister. He said that there would be no harm in calling you for visit. He reiterated that we must succeed, as that will have far reaching effect on further development. Well, that is why you are here. Now the rest is up to you. Incidentally, the involvement of Dukhia has to be kept as confidential, that is what the minister had told me."

"I must meet Dukhia first," said Akshay.

"That has been arranged; he will be here in the evening."

Akshay was most delighted to meet Dukhia after so many years. For an hour they talked about their days in Lonavala. Dukhia had gone old past seventy years but he was fit, full of exuberance.

Dhukhia said, "Marathi Sahib, I feel so happy that you have come. I wanted to do something for my people and now that you have come I feel confident that I would be successful. My people believe that prosperity would come when some prominent person like you visits our village and shows us the way."

"There is nothing great about me. Now tell me what should I do for you?"

"Give us *darshan*[1]," said Dukhia. "Our people in the village want to see you and so do the tribals living in the adjacent areas."

"That part is OK but do you know that I do not specialize in breeding table fishes? This job is being done by Dorabji Trust."

"I know that. I have been to their fish farms and met the concerned officials. They did not impress me. I asked for you because of your personality. You alone have that ability to make an impact on people. The first impression is important."

"Look Dukhia, my going to your village would amount to encroachment in somebody else's field. The GM of Dorabji may not like it. Besides, I would not be of any help to you; the

---

1. Sight, View.

assistance has to be provided by him."

"I understand that but yours is going to be one time visit, after that we will manage with Dorabji. We will not trouble you again."

"The general manager of Dorabji told me that the social situation in your area is not congenial. Your Thakur has dictatorial habits and he is a very difficult person."

"That is correct, but leave that to us. It is our problem and we will sort it out. We need your help only in one respect and that is, you must visit us."

Akshay spoke to GM of Dorabji. He told him about his conversation with Dukhia. He asked him in a forthright manner if he would mind his going to Khajaria. The GM told him, "Not at all, go ahead. The taxi for you has been arranged tomorrow morning. I would advise you to stop for half an hour at Darbangha and visit our fish farm."

Akshay before going to sleep was thinking about his impending visit. If it were not for Dukhia, he would have never agreed to go. Once he had asked him—

"Why were you named as *Dukhia*[1]?"

"My parent's successively lost three children soon after their birth. They named me Dukhia hoping that I would survive."

Dukhia was born as a healthy baby and grew up in that fashion. He was hard working and never felt tired. He lost his parents in his adolescence and had to fend for himself. He did not marry and led a single life. He was grateful to God for the job he had got. His attachment to his village was strong. He went there every year to meet his people.

Akshay had asked him about his ambition in life. He said that he would like to do something concrete in his village for the good of the people.

Next morning Akshay and Dukhia proceeded by taxi to the

1. A-person afflicted with grief.

village. They reached Darbangha after five hours of drive and visited the fish farm as advised by the GM. He was pleased to see their work in production of spawns, their development into fry and nurture up to the stage of fingerling. The unit was modern and hygienic. They produced adequate quantities of fingerlings for distribution to village ponds in the district.

The road from Darbangha to Khajaria was unmetalled. They got into fishery's jeep and reached the village by evening. Akshay spent the night in the village. Dukhia had gone out of the way to make him comfortable.

The following day was busy for Akshay. Early in the morning, he went round the area and had a look at various *pokhras*[1] in and around the village. Thereafter he saw a few large ponds and a big reservoir in the tribal area. He found them suitable.

The area had a look of poverty. The land holding of farmers was small, not enough to support the family. The competent and able-bodied youth had migrated to the cities, all over the country, to earn money while the old and indolent had remained behind. Much of their livelihood depended upon the remittance sent by their relatives.

Akshay returned by lunchtime and managed two hours of rest.

In the afternoon, Dukhia had arranged an assembly of village people and the tribals. Akshay addressed them and explained to them the benefit of breeding fish in simplest words without using any jargons and technical terms. He told them, "The occurrence of fishes in ponds and rivers is a natural process. Every year the fishes lay eggs in large numbers. They get hatched and the small fishes in due course of time grow into big fishes. The fishes feed on weeds for which we have to do nothing.

Today we have reached a stage where our ponds do not have any fishes. Why? It is because of our ignorance, negligence and lack of understanding. The fishes should never be netted

1. Ponds.

during their breeding season from September to December. But we don't follow that. The fishes should be allowed to grow for two to three years, so that they can lay eggs. Here again, we don't do that. And that is how the fishes have disappeared. The net result is that our ponds are left with only trash fishes, which we do not eat.

Let me now explain what the fisheries do for you. They collect eggs from healthy grown up fishes. From these eggs, they hatch the delicate newly born fishes and allow them to grow up to the size of our fingers. These finger size fishes are strong enough to be dropped in the ponds. They are free from all diseases and can feed on the weeds. This is the most difficult part of fish breeding and it is done for you by the fisheries.

All that you have to do is not catch them for first six months to a year. Thereafter you can catch them by net but the net must have holes, big enough to allow small fishes to escape. You will do a great good if you do not catch fishes during their breeding season.

Fish breeding does not need hard manual labour. It does not need education and specialised training; one can learn by experience. Women can do the work equally well. The most advantageous aspect of fish breeding is that it is a part time occupation and does not interfere with your other work."

The village audience was impressed by his simple and straight talk. There was charisma in his manners and speech. The meeting ended in an hour's time with people cheering, '*Marathi Sahib ki Jai*[1].' Dukhia was most happy; his master's talk had made the desired impact on the people.

Dukhia took Akshay to Zamindar's *haveli*[2]. On the way, he told him that the Thakur is very fond of his voice, he does not like any argument and interruption; the best thing is to listen to him and keep quiet. Thakur welcomed his guest and said,

"The people here are ignorant; they don't understand that

---

1. Cheers to the Marathi Sahib.
2. Mansion, a big house.

the fishes have to be protected. If the scheme is left under my control, I assure you and your department that the fishes would be safe.

Our people are backward but they are well meaning. They are docile and well behaved; they do not indulge in agitation, slogan shouting etc. The place is peaceful and there is no police post here.

When you go back, you can tell your department to send fingerlings. I must tell you that our *Sarpanch*[1] is a trained hand. He has worked in fishery near Mumbai for more than thirty years. You can tell them that I will take personal interest and ensure that fish breeding is successful."

Akshay heard the landlord patiently. There were inconsistencies in his talk but he did not open his mouth. The Thakur was pleased.

Around 8 P.M. in the night, two tribal chiefs came to see him. Dukhia told his master that the meeting was important. They were his protectors and he relied very heavily on them.

The tribal chiefs said that they would like development of fishery in their area. Over the years the produce from the forest and land has gone down and therefore fish breeding has become important for their survival. The tribal people are disciplined, they do not have any problem of ownership and the produce is shared by all.

Akshay told them that he has all sympathies for them. If the scheme is successful in Khajaria, it will be extended to their area in no time. The government is very keen to help them but Khajaria must succeed.

The two chiefs assured Akshay that in their own interest they would see to it that fish breeding in Khajaria was successful.

Akshay had done the job as desired by his old mali. Next morning he was on his way back. Dukhia accompanied him up to Darbangha and thereafter he proceeded alone.

---

1. Head of the village council.

During the return flight, Akshay was thinking about his visit to Khajaria. He recalled that Dukhia had often told him that the developments, which had taken place in Maharashtra, should take root in his native place. His visit was hectic but if it gave impetus to rural and tribal development, it was worth the trouble.

From the beginning Dukhia used to call him as Marathi Sahib. He was amused by the cheering of Marathi Sahib ki Jai. Did he do anything extraordinary to earn such applause? Hardly any. The facts were that when the British came they brought education, administration and social development to the three presidencies of East India Company and later it spread to the other states. There was a time when the city of Kolkata alone had medical colleges, while many states in North India did not have even one. The educated people from the three presidencies of Bombay, Madras and Calcutta moved to adjoining states on lucrative jobs and the locals called them as sahibs. Over the years the situation had changed but the disparity remained for a long time.

Disparity is not desirable. There is a disparity between urban and rural areas and it is most glaring when it comes to tribal areas. Akshay was resolved to help backward regions and if he was able to do that, he certainly would be proud of being Marathi and the acclaim— Marathi Sahib ki Jai.

Akshay was distressed about the movement of *Marathi Manus*[1]. It was bringing bad name to Maharashtra. It was time that Maharashtrians concentrate their attention on problems within; the state had already slipped from its number one position and was going from bad to worse.

Akshay had returned to Lonavala. After three months he contacted GM of Dorabji. The latter told him that the fingerlings have been sent to Khajaria in his transport and have been put in the pond. He was happy that the beginning had been made.

He had complied with the request of Dukhia. Would he

1. Marathi people.

succeed? Dukhia must have tied up all loose ends. But would he be able to overcome Thakur's obstinacy? When he had gone to haveli, he had noticed ruffians at the entrance gate and inside the house. That was something which was worrying him.

Dukhia was aware of his problems. He had told Akshay not to bother about the internal situation, it concerned him and it was up to him to sort them out. The awakening was taking place and the people wanted their involvement and say in the village affairs. Thakur was opposed to it; he wanted his overlordship to continue. Dukhia was doing the balancing act. He maintained a good working relationship with both. He knew that the Thakur had employed tough looking bodyguards in his service and the village had no answer to them. To make matters worse, the bodyguards were enrolled from outside and had no sympathy with the villagers. They were not allowed to bring families and lived single. To counter them, Dukhia had cultivated friendship with tribal chiefs for succour. He had met the leaders of the political party in power. The minister for fisheries had assured him for all possible help provided that initiative came from the village. Someone had to take lead, mobilise people and make a sacrifice.

By June the fishes were five month old. Occasionally they used to jump up on the surface of the water and send ripples around. The children were seeing them for the first time and were thrilled to watch the scene.

Thakur Mahavir Singh had called Dukhia and the five representatives of the people to his mansion. His bodyguards had told him certain unpalatable things.

"I am told that you have formed a cooperative society. Why did you do that?"

"That was precondition for getting fingerlings. We had no other choice."

"And you have also organised self help group of women!"

"That was done to get cheap labour."

Thakur was visibly annoyed. He took time to recompose himself. He told the village representatives, "What you have done will never succeed. It is just not practical. The efforts made by the cooperative societies and the governments invariably fail and that is because of absence of personal involvement. You can blame businessmen and contractors for exploitation and extraction of work, but they succeed.

I have a feeling that you people have been carried away by mistaken ideals. Very soon you will realize the blunder that you have made. That would occur when the fishes are ready for catch. That's the time when people will start fighting with each other for their share and poachers will become active. You have no solution for that. That's the time you will come to me for help. And I will not help you because you have neglected me."

Dukhia pleaded, "Sarkar if you permit me, may I say a few words. Actually, we started the scheme as a trial. We thought that we should come to you only after we succeed. You are right; the trouble will start when the fishes grow up. We would need your help and that of your bodyguards to deal with miscreants and poachers. We are not going to neglect you. We have decided to send you four best fishes out of every catch from each pond as a gesture of our appreciation for protection and order. When all the five ponds produce fish, you will get twenty fishes from every catch and that would be sufficient for your house and the guards."

Dukhia asked other representatives, "Am I right?" They nodded their head.

Thakur was shrewd. There was a meaning in what the Sarpanch had said. Let the trial succeed before he acts. The ponds had been without fish for more than fifty years.

Thakur had two grown up sons and a daughter. They lived in Patna. Every year, his sons and daughter went to their village during Diwali. That was a great occasion for Thakur and his wife.

Thakur had called Sarpanch for distribution of work for the festival. The haveli needed cleaning up and white washing. That was an annual requirement of the landlord and Dukhia knew the details of work to be done.

"How are the fishes doing?"

"They are growing up well. Most of them are more than half kg in weight."

"I will need fishes when my sons and daughter come."

"Sure," said Dukhia with a smile.

Dukhia was waiting in the courtyard of the haveli with a bag in his hand. The younger son of Thakur came out. Unlike his father, he was polite in his behaviour. He greeted Dukhia, "*Sarpanch ji Ram, Ram.*[1]"

Dukhia got up, "*Pai lagi, Chote Sarkar.*[2]"

"What have you brought in the bag?"

"Fish, fresh from the pond."

Vinay did not look pleased. "Don't you know that you are not supposed to catch fish during their breeding season?"

By that time, the Thakur and his elder son had also come out. Vinay told his father about the mistake committed by the Sarpanch.

His father said that he had asked for it. It was a festive time and the fishes were big enough to eat.

"The trouble in our country is that the major festivals like Navratri, Durgapuja, Dussera and Diwali occur during their breeding season. We catch fishes and prevent them from multiplying. It is the fish eaters who have to exercise control. If we don't eat, the fishes will not be sold and therefore they will not be caught. I ask you, what difference would it make? During these months, we can always eat mutton or chicken."

Dukhia tried to pacify Vinay. "*Chote Sarkar*[3], we get fingerlings from the fish farm and therefore it would not make

---

1. A form of greeting to elders or superiors.
2. Return of greetings by subordinates.
3. Young master.

much difference. Besides, the fish is a delicacy and has a different taste."

"Sarpanch ji, you are not getting my point. In the name of religion, we observe fast, restraint and self-control. Here, it is a simple case of commonsense. Now do me a favour. Please take the fishes away. You can give them to dogs or cats but don't give it to human beings."

The people in the village were happy with the views expressed by Vinay. Many times when the people were unhappy with the rude and atrocious behaviour of Thakur, Dukhia used to advise them to show patience. A time must come when Thakur Mahavir Singh would go away from the scene. Vinay and his elder brother were very considerate and they would bring happy days for them.

An evening before returning to Patna, Vinay told his father that he must change his dictatorial habits. Social awakening has taken place and very soon it will come to their village. The elder brother told his father that it was time that he should quit the village and settle down in Patna. "We and our children are not going to live in Khajaria and therefore there is no point in sticking on. You must also remember that you have gone old. We cannot look after you and mother from such a long distance."

Thakur Mahavir Singh was debating in his mind. Vinay had told him about the awareness amongst the people; there was nothing new in that. He had advised him to change his dictatorial habits but surely he was not a dictator! Admittedly he was strict and at times abusive but people don't work unless they get a kick. Vijay had advised him to leave the village and settle down in Patna. How could he do that? The property and land was worth a fortune. It was his ancestral property and ownership of land was a status symbol. The area was backward but he was confident that development would come soon. Metalled road would be constructed, the area will get electrified;

school, hospital, post office and bank would come up in the next five years. He was only sixty-two and therefore he could wait. Unlike Vijay, the younger son Vinay was not averse to rural life. He pinned his hope on Vinay for continuity and decided to leave behind a solid estate for him. He dismissed the thought of going to Patna.

His major concern was safety and security. The days of loyalty and respect on the part of poor and subordinates were over. The joint family had disappeared and he and his wife living alone were vulnerable. He did not get good sleep in the nights and took calmpose before going to bed. His sons brought the medicine whenever they came from Patna. There was a strong reason for him to employ bodyguards. In addition, he kept firearms with him for protection.

Towards the end of December, Thakur got a call from Vijay stating that his son and daughter had developed fever, cough and cold. This time it was severe. His wife became restless; she went to Patna under escort. Before leaving, she gave detailed instructions to the housemaid to look after the master.

Next month Dukhia went to haveli. He carried four fishes with him. He told Malik that the fish-breeding season was over and they had caught a few fishes for sample. Thakur had a good look at them; they were nearly one kg in weight and appeared healthy. He smiled.

"That's a splendid work. Are you satisfied with the trial?"

"Yes Sarkar."

"Are you ready for expansion?"

"Absolutely."

Thakur thought for a while and disclosed his ideas on fish breeding to Dukhia. "I am thinking of forming a company with myself as head and some of you people as members. I will provide capital and take the responsibility of protecting the fishes. My guards will patrol the area. We have five big and equal numbers of small ponds. The profit will be shared equitably; 50% to myself and the rest to shareholders. It will generate employment in the village and provide them cheap fish. What do you think?"

'I will discuss it in *panchayat*[1]."

"Do that and come back to me."

Dukhia went back to the landlord after a fortnight. He told Thakur that the people are not willing to follow his suggestion.

"Why?"

"They say that the pokharas are common property. They want to breed fish as equal partners."

"Common property!" Thakur frowned. "They have conveniently forgotten that my forefathers were the captors of this area. The land and all that grows or exists on it was their property. They brought in the first batch of landless, poor peasants and gave them land for cultivation and the facility of water. Look at the ingratitude of these people; they are now claiming it as common property!"

"Sarkar, what you say is a fact. But the people are getting obsessed with freedom. Already they have got the land in their names and now they are claiming ownership of ponds. Some of them have met political leaders. The politicians are inciting them. They have affirmed that ponds cannot be treated as private property."

"Look Dukhia, I am not claiming pokharas as my private property. I possibly cannot deny people drinking water, a place for ablution etc but they should use their sense. I had already told you that the cooperative societies don't succeed; they invariably fail. Why do they want to take a risk? I am telling them something for their own good."

"Sarkar, I will speak to them once again and come back to you."

Sarpanch once again discussed the proposal made by

---

1. The body of five elected persons.

Thakur in the *gram sabha.*[1] It was not agreed to. He told Thakur about the response of the people.

"What do they say?"

"Fish breeding is being sponsored by the government as cooperative venture by the villagers. They want to pursue it accordingly. They want to launch the project in a big way after *Phagua.*[2]"

Mahavir Singh had to take action and that too very soon before the return of his wife. He had dreamt of getting into fish business in a big way and had eyed the lucrative market of Kolkata. This was something which he wanted to leave behind for his sons. If the cooperative society venture succeeds it would be too late for him. The time was now.

He called the two leaders of his bodyguards and told them about the rebellious behaviour of the villagers. They told him that they had also heard something of that sort in the village gossip.

"We must not permit them to succeed. They want to launch their project after Phagua."

The two leaders smiled. "*Malik*[3] if you allow us, we will play this year's Holi with blood."

"Don't you do that? The idea is to teach them a lesson to accept sensible proposal which I have made."

"Malik, we are at your service. Tell us what you want us to do and it will be done."

"In every group there are a few front runners. Identify them. If they are given a lesson, the rest will fall in line. Find out their details and come back to me within three days."

The guards identified Sarpanch, the five representatives of the village council and a dozen wrestlers of *Akhara*[4]. The head of Akhara was Balram. Besides wrestling, he used to train his disciples in the use of *Lathi*[5].

---

1. Vallage assembly.
2. Holi.
3. Master, lord.
4. A ground made for wrestling.
5. Bamboo stick.

Thakur was pleased. "Now this is what you have to do. You will not kill anyone, nor will you break bones or cripple any one. Give them a good beating and that is about all. Be careful about Dukhia. He is as much my man as theirs. He must not be hurt. Tell them to follow my advice. Would you be able to identify these rebels in the night?"

"Yes Malik. That should not be a problem."

The day was fixed two days later and time at midnight.

Dhanna was the most trusted servant of the haveli liked by Thakur and his wife. She had been working there for the last twenty five years. She became a widow at the age of fourteen, a week after her marriage. The in-laws treated her as sinner responsible for their son's death. She was fed up with ill treatment and wanted to end her life. She went to Dukhia for help. The latter met the father of present Thakur. He was old and wanted someone reliable to look after him. She was employed and a place was given to her to live in the house. She found a new lease of life and was happy.

The trouble for her started ten years later after the death of the old man. Mahavir Singh started eying her and took advantage of her helpless situation. She acquiesced and did not say anything. She did not inform Dukhia or anyone else. Sometimes she used to smile out of contempt on her fate. Mahavir took her smile as a sign of consent.

She held Dukhia in the highest esteem. She could not accept any harm being done to him. She informed him about the plan hatched in the haveli for beating the ring leaders.

Balram was a cool *pahalwan*[1]. He told his followers and the representatives of people to come to him after dusk. Dukhia did not turn up. He took them to a shelter and briefed them about their role.

In the haveli, Thakur was feeling restless. He opened a bottle

1. Wrestler.

of liquor and poured a drink. He called Dhanna,

"What have you made for dinner?"

"Chicken, vegetable and *dal*[1]."

"Good. Make *parathas*[2]."

Dhanna smiled and that pleased Thakur. He drank leisurely till such time he felt a bit tipsy. Around ten in the night, he told Dhanna to bring food. He pulled her close and started kissing and fondling her body. "Not now, let's do it after dinner," said Dhanna with a smile. It suited him; he had to keep awake for a few more hours.

That night Dhanna was very sweet to him. She remained with him throughout the dinner and served him food with inviting gestures till such time that he was full. After dinner, she put her arms around his waist, led him to the bed and kissed him passionately. She told him to wait; she would be back in no time after her meals.

Thakur was worked up. He took off his clothes and covered himself with a sheet. He was waiting for Dhanna.

Dhanna was in no hurry. Leisurely she had her meals, cleaned up the kitchen and went to Thakur's room. He was lying naked in the bed and was snoring. What he did not know was that she had put plenty of sleeping pills in the spicy chicken curry. She went out of the room and waited till the bodyguards left the haveli on their mission.

The private army of the Thakur first went to the hut of Sarpanch. They dragged him out and gave him a light dressing. They told him that this was the first dose of things to follow if he did not comply with the wishes of Malik.

Thereafter they went in search of others. To their surprise they found that the offenders on their list were missing. They threatened the villagers of dire consequence if they did not disclose their hideout. A meek looking old man told them that

1. A dish prepared from pulses.
2. Fried chapati.

the whole lot were hiding in the corner hut and pointed the direction.

The bodyguards boldly walked towards the hut. They were going through an alley. In front of the hut they found two carts, which blocked the approach to the hut. The carts were loaded with hay. When they started climbing the carts, the loose hay was slipping under their feet and at the same time they came under a volley of lathis from Balram and his followers. They were stranded in a hopeless situation; the alley was narrow and not more than four men at a time could take part in the assault. The two leaders of guards felt frustrated but something else had occurred behind them, which threatened them more seriously.

They saw two *mashals*[1] at the other end of the alley. The two tribal chiefs with sixty members of their clan had reached the site; they were armed with bows, arrows and lances. The valiant army of the Thakur was sandwiched between Balram's men and the tribal force. There was no way to escape and they surrendered meekly.

Balram and his men came out of the hut. The bodyguards were made to lie prostrate on the ground. Their hands and feet were tied with ropes. The tribal chiefs, the five representatives of the village and Balram went to meet Sarpanch leaving the captives in the charge of Balram's men and the tribal force.

Dhanna returned to Thakur's room. He was snoring in deep sleep. She shook him with both her hands but he did not wake up.

She sat on a chair and watched Thakur. She was wild with his action to send his bodyguards to beat Dukhia and the villagers. She could have forgiven Thakur for illicit relations but she could not tolerate any harm being done to her mentor. Once when she was fed up of life and wanted to commit suicide, Dukhia had advised her to be brave. He had told her to use

---

1. Torch.

her life in service of others and that's what she was going to do now.

Thakur kept weapons in the room for his protection. She took out revolver, had a good look and kept it back. The shot will make unnecessary noise. She picked up a *khanjar*[1] and thrust it in his stomach with full force. Thakur groaned for a while and lay motionless with blood streaming out of his belly.

It was time for her to end her own life. She had a last contemptuous look at the Thakur. Here was a man who was making use of her for the last fifteen years in total anonymity. No one knew about his wickedness, not even his wife. She did not disclose it to Dukhia as that would have hurt his feelings. "Let them know it now," she said to herself. She picked up a *khukri*[2], threw off her clothes and knelt naked by his side. She gripped the handle firmly in her hands and pierced the point in her stomach. Thereafter she fell flat on the sharp weapon and was gone forever.

The five representatives, the two tribal chiefs and Balram had reached Dukhia's hut. He was lightly beaten and no bodily injury was caused to him. He could move his limbs and talk.

They discussed their next course of action. Balram said that Thakur without his aides was meaningless and therefore we should get rid of them. The tribal chiefs said that they could take away the bodyguards to their area and finish them.

Dukhia heard their views. He said, "Don't you forget our aim. We want to get going with fish breeding. If any law and order situation is created at this point of time, our project will be affected and it will never take off. Surely, we don't want that!

Think coolly. All that has happened is that I have received minor beating and that is not very serious. No one has been injured. The best course for us is to negotiate with Thakur and remember that we are now in a position of strength. We must

---

1. Dagger.
2. A sharp curved weapon like dagger.

insist that his bodyguard should be sacked and thrown out of the village. Thakur must agree to our terms."

He sent two representatives to the haveli to meet Thakur. When they returned, they told Sarpanch about the death of Thakur and Dhanna.

Dukhia smiled to himself. He said, "Our problems are over in one stroke but we have to be careful. We should expect arrival of police and Thakur's family. We will not have any problems with Chote Sarkars. Vinay Bhaiyya had told me that when his time comes, he would get rid of guards and the false sense of security."

In the meantime, the bodyguards were pushed to an open area. They were huddled together and made to sit on their haunches. Round them, the tribal group were dancing, clasping their hands and pointing their lances at them. The scene was terror-ridden under the flickering light of mashals.

The tribal chiefs thumped the ground with their lances. That was a signal for the tribals to stop dance. Balram told the guards about the murder of Thakur. "What punishment do you want?"

The bodyguards begged mercy. They were willing to do anything if their lives were spared.

Balram told them that they should never enter their village ever again. Mockingly he told them that with the death of Thakur, they have lost their jobs. They should not divulge this incident to anyone and under no circumstances make a report to the police. If they agreed to this condition, it might be possible for him to plead to the village council for their safe exit.

The punishment was lenient to which the bodyguards readily agreed. Balram told them to wait for further instructions.

Dukhia thanked the tribal chiefs for their help. He told them that the tribal force could return to their area. They should take the bodyguards with them and keep them under captivity till such time the police investigations are over. He requested the two chiefs to remain behind for some more time.

After the death of Thakur, a very heavy responsibility had fallen on the shoulders of Sarpanch. He along with others proceeded to the haveli.

He found the mobile of Thakur and rang up two chote sarkars. Vinay told him that he was starting straightway. On the way he would inform the police station at Darbangha. Vijay told him that he would take some time as his mother, wife and children would need time to get ready. He also has to bring his sister and Vinay's wife.

Dukhia went into Thakur's room. The scene was disgusting. He came out and locked the door. The naked bodies would spread rumours and bad name. It occurred to him that this act must have been performed by Dhanna but why did she do that? He had no answer. He was thinking of what he should do? He decided to wait for the arrival of Vinay.

He asked his colleagues if the news of murder had spread to the village. They said, 'No'. He told them to maintain silence and wait for the arrival of chote sarkars.

Vinay reached by midday. Dukhia briefed him about the tragedy and escorted him to Thakur's room. Vinay was shocked to see the scene. It looked as if they had killed each other or committed suicide. The sight of naked bodies was disturbing. He told Dukhia that this would bring a bad name to their family.

"You are right, Chote Sarkar," said Dhukia. "I have been thinking about it since morning. I am glad that you have come. We need your advice on what should we do?"

"Let me think. What have you thought?"

"Let us put clothes on them. Dhanna's body should be taken to the kitchen. That would suggest that the murder was done by dacoits."

"We can open the locker, remove its contents and keep the door open," said Vinay. "What should we do about the weapons?"

"They can be removed and disposed off."

Vinay said that the police was likely to reach in two hour's time. We should be quick. The work was executed promptly. Khukari and Khanjar were removed and given to the tribal chiefs. Dukhia told them that their work was over and they too could go back.

The police had reached haveli. They examined the dead bodies and the locker. They searched the mansion for sharp edged weapons or any clues left behind by the dacoits. They recorded the evidence of those present and took three hours to complete their investigation. By that time Vijay had arrived with all other members of the family.

The inspector asked, "Would you like a post mortem to be carried out?"

"That is up to you," said Vijay. " But I would like to say that tomorrow will be earliest for post mortem and that would mean that cremation can take place only day after. By that time the body will get thoroughly decomposed and stink."

"I see your point," the inspector said. "Post mortem can be dispensed with if we record the consent of all next of kin and heirs of the deceased."

"That should not be difficult, all of us are here."

The haveli was grief stricken. They decided to do the cremation next day. Vijay asked, "Where are our bodyguards?"

"They ran away out of sense of guilt when they learnt about the death of Thakur."

The entire village was present to pay homage and witness the last rites of their Malik. Dukhia alone remembered Dhanna; she had suffered in her life.

Vijay left after fifteen days. Vinay stayed on for a month. He told his mother to come to Patna. She declined; the haveli cannot be left unoccupied. Her main problem was loss of Dhanna. Over the years she had got used to her.

Dukhia assured that *Thakurain*[1] would be looked after. He had in mind a suitable maid for her. The entire village was at her call. Balram and his men would look after the security of the haveli. They are from the village and therefore more reliable.

Phagua, the most popular festival, was celebrated in low key because of the tragedy. A week later, Vinay performed a *pooja*[2] for the success of fish breeding and fingerlings were dropped in all ponds.

The minister for fisheries had learnt about the enthusiasm evinced by the people of Khajaria and the tribal region. He visited them six months later and was impressed by their efforts. He met the chief minister and apprised him about the initiative taken by the people.

Development of the backward regions and removal of disparity was on top of chief minister's agenda.

"How can I help them?"

"Sanction road and other utility works."

In Lonavala, Akshay had received a letter calling him to Patna as a member of selection committee. He was happy with the prospect of meeting Dukhia. He was periodically getting news about his success and three years had passed since he had met him last.

Akshay had decided to give a surprise visit. When he crossed Darbangha, he was moving on a tarmac road. He could see the works being done on electrification.

In a village like Khajaria, a visit by car was not common. The children surrounded him and some of the villagers recognised Marathi Sahib. Dukhia welcomed him. "I am glad that this time you have come on your own without being called."

"I had heard so much about your great efforts. I felt that I must see them."

Akshay was lodged in the haveli. Vinay had permanently

---

1. Wife of Thakur.
2. Worship.

shifted to the village. Akshay liked the pleasant manners of Vinay, most unlike his father. They spent the evening together in talks; Vinay was widely read with many hobbies.

Vinay said, "You are still calling him as Dukhia. We have changed his name; he is now called as *Sukhia*[1]."

"Well, well. It was his life's ambition to distribute happiness to others."

Next morning Akshay was taken round the area. Vinay and Sukhia were with him. The fish-breeding programme had taken off well and Akshay congratulated Sukhia for his outstanding performance. The village was showing the signs of development.

They went to the tribal region. Akshay stopped for a long time at a particular reservoir. It was a huge lake surrounded by low hills. There was no habitation nearby. Akshay took many photographs.

"It looks that not many people visit this place," said Akshay.

"There is nothing here to attract them."

"The place is beautiful; people could settle here."

"That is not possible. The tribal people do not like intrusion in their area. They want to retain their isolation and identity."

"All these are plus points," said Akshay.

"I don't understand what you are saying," said Vinay.

Akshay smiled. "Look, in a developing country like ours, fish for food has to be the first priority. We will go through that. There is something, which people have not realised as yet. Fishing is an excellent sport and Mahseer is an angler's dream. If we start now it will take ten years."

"I am with you," said Vinay.

1. Opposite of Dukhia, one who is happy.

SULOCHANA

It was a special day for Sulochana, her 85th birthday. Her entire family comprising of two sons, three daughters, their spouses and grandchildren had gathered to wish her happy birthday. It was difficult for twenty two people to stay in the flat but despite inconvenience they decided to huddle and stay together on this happy occasion.

The old lady lived in the corner room under constant care of a nurse. Sharp at 7 P.M. the nurse brought her in the drawing room in a wheel chair. She was donning an expensive silk sari and her face was powdered and freshened up for the event. One by one everyone came to greet her and expressed their best wishes to Akka, the name by which she was called. In turn she gave a present to each of her loved ones. She cut the cake and the joyous assembly sang 'Happy Birthday.'

For an hour Sulochana sat in the midst of her relatives. Her memory was failing and she could not recognise most of them. She was confusing names and relationship. She recognised her eldest son Suresh, his wife Shalini and grandson Nakul; that was because she lived with them in the flat. It was difficult for her near and dear ones to comprehend what all was going on in her mind, but she looked happy with so many people around her. She ate a piece of cake and little *Khichari*[1]. She felt

1. A light diet of boiled rice and pulse.

tired and went to sleep. The nurse took her back to the room and closed the door.

The much awaited party began thereafter. It was after five years that the family of Ranvade had got together, the last one was the eightieth birthday. Suresh had taken pains to organise the party in the best possible manner. Drinks, snacks and food were lavish, to please every one's taste. The birthday party went on till late, past midnight.

Next morning the family members got up late recalling the excellent party, which they had on the previous night. Their happy mood was however upset and spirits dampened by something that was said by their eldest brother and his wife. They were planning to go to US for four months. They wanted someone to look after the mother during their absence. There was silence in the room and no one volunteered. The relatives left for their respective places and by evening the flat in Sonewadi was back to normal.

Suresh's younger brother Amon lived in Pune and his three sisters— Kamini, Madhavi and Padmini lived in Mumbai, Bangalore and Chennai. All of them except Amon led a comfortable and decent life. Amon could not do well compared to others and lived in a small flat. Suresh wanted to go to US, his daughter had been calling her parents, but then there was a problem of Akka, who would look after her? Amon's flat was too small, he was not in a position to look after her and the sisters were engrossed in their own affairs. But Shalini was insistent; why can't they look after her for a few months? Her husband did not know how to manage the trip. The vexed problem got resolved in a queer manner. Akka had called Suresh next morning; she told him that she was not going to live very long and she would like to spend her last days in her own flat.

Shalini asked, "How did Akka get to know that we are planning to go to US and she will have to spend a few months somewhere else?

Suresh told her that he did not tell Akka anything about their plan of going abroad. Even if he had told her it was doubtful if she could have recalled anything. I suppose, she must have got a hunch of her coming end.

Shalini was not very pleased; she bit her lips in frustration and said, "For the time being we can postpone our going but go we must."

Suresh had noted that his son was absent in the party. He asked—

"Where were you yesterday? I did not see you. You jolly well knew that it was Akka's 85th birthday. You should have been present in the party!"

"Whose party?" Nakul quipped. "Akka's party was over at 8 P.M. when she was taken to her room; I was present till that time."

"But your uncle and aunts were there."

"I talked to them for an hour. All of you were looking happy amongst yourselves and I wonder if anyone was missing me. Look, I must tell you where I went. My friend Vinay got engaged yesterday and I had to attend it. He had called me at seven; I could not do that and went at nine. Actually I attended both, Akka's birthday and my friend's engagement. Did I do anything wrong?"

Suresh kept quiet.

Nakul asked, "Tell me, what happened about your plans for going to US? Did anyone volunteer to look after Akka?"

"We have postponed it for the time being."

Nakul gave a mischievous smile and went away.

Sulochana belonged to Pune. She had married Mahadev who was employed in Nasik. That is where her five children were born. Her husband died at the age of fifty when the children were still in school and college going age. She decided to sell the house in Nasik and settle down in Pune where better facilities were available for education. Her relatives were in Pune and they helped her to buy a flat in Sonewadi.

For many years she led a difficult life struggling with the situation. She had to look after two boys and three girls, singlehanded within the limited means. Suresh did graduation in commerce and thereafter CA. He took up a job at the age of twenty-five and that greatly relieved her. In due course the girls completed their education. They were well behaved and beautiful. The suitors came to the house seeking betrothal and their marriages did not pose her any problem. Amon was not sharp and active; he gave up studies after B.A. and managed to get a job of a school teacher. Sulochana was not very happy with his performance but she reconciled; one does not get everything in life and what she had got was enough.

Suresh did not marry till such time that his sisters were married. His boss, the secretary of the company liked him immensely and offered his daughter for marriage. Shalini liked him for his polite behaviour.

The last problem for Sulochana was to settle Amon. She selected a down to earth girl from a middle class family. She was teaching in a school and Akka felt that the match would be ideal. She told Suresh to search a flat for Amon.

"Don't you want him and his wife to stay here with you?"

"I do, but it would be better if they stay separately."

"How do we get that much of money?"

"Leave that to me. Look for a small flat, it would be easier for them to maintain."

Sulochana was shrewd. She knew that frictions take place between daughters in-law. Shalini's father had offered dowry at the time of marriage. She did not take it at that time and had told him to keep that amount aside.

Amon was married and he shifted to the new flat. The two brothers and particularly their wives got precisely what they had wished and they thanked Akka for the foresight.

Sulochana had gone through the long period of trials and tribulation and had finally overcome all her problems. Her next thirty years were happy; her sons and daughters were managing their affairs well, they lived amicably and met her periodically. She spent most of her time in recollecting the past incidents. She spent considerable time on worship and followed religious observances.

She kept good health. When she was 75, she told her sons to find a place for her in the home for the aged, where she could spend her remaining years. She did not like to be a burden on them. Her sons laughed at the idea.

"Akka, you are hale and hearty. Your medical reports are clear. You don't have any problems."

"But I will have them soon. I do not want to tie you down."

Her sons did not agree and she continued to live on in the house. She made a WILL stating that her assets should be utilised for her maintenance until death and thereafter to be shared equally by her sons and daughters. She donated her body for medical research and organs for the needy.

When she was eighty she fell ill. It took three months for her to recover. She went through extensive examination. The doctors declared that all her vital organs were functioning satisfactorily and there was no cause for alarm. But Sulochana was upset. She had become feeble and dependent; she needed help for walking and going to the toilet. Suresh employed a daytime nurse for her.

Sulochana told her sons to send her to some *Ashram*[1] in Kashi, Prayag or Haridwar. She expressed desire to spend her last days on the banks of Ganga. Her sons did not agree. They recalled the sacrifices made by her and vowed to be with her until the last.

Akka was not happy. On a piece of paper she wrote that in her life she had seen good days and bad days, she was fully satisfied with her life, there was no meaning in her existence

1. Hermitage.

and she did not want to live any more. She put the paper in an envelope and gave it to Suresh. Her sons read the letter. They became apprehensive that Akka may commit suicide. They removed all sharp objects from her room and strong medicines. A separate nurse was employed for night duty. The nurses were instructed to keep a watch on her lest she did something untoward to her life.

Years back, Nakul had advised his father to keep Akka in a home for the aged. Now that the grandmother had gone senile, what difference did it make whether she lived in hospital, *vridhashram*[1] or the house? He blamed his father for being emotional instead of being practical.

Shalini had been reminding her husband about their visit to America. Her husband was dilly-dallying. Nakul told her that papa would never be able to go. The practical solution was that the two of them should go and let him remain behind to attend to his mother.

Shalini wanted her husband to accompany otherwise Sheela would feel offended. She had got a job after four years of hard work for doing M.B.A. It was difficult for her to get any leave in the near future and therefore she wanted them to go to US.

Nakul told her, "That part is OK but we know father's attachment to Akka. It would be futile to persuade him. No one else would take the responsibility of looking after Akka in our absence and if we keep on postponing, we will never make it."

Finally Shalini and her son went to US. She was fond of travelling and good things of life, and that was despite her weight and diabetes. Their journey to America was trouble free. Sheela received them at the airport. She had acquired a two-bedroom flat, neatly furnished. The three of them enjoyed every moment of their being together. Sheela took them to places for sightseeing, picnics and weekend outings. Shalini liked the

1. Home for the aged.

change; in Pune she had felt like a nurse on duty.

Shalini had gone to a nearby store for shopping. She made leisurely purchases and the bag became heavy. While crossing the road, she slipped and a speeding van instantly crushed her to death.

After the initial shock, Sheela said that she must make arrangements to send the dead body to India. Nakul told her that there would be no point in doing that. The cremation rites, here or in Pune, would have to be performed by him. Los Angeles is a big city with large Indian population and the facility of *Guruji*[1] was available. The children talked to their father and he agreed.

On return Nakul narrated the details to his father. Suresh was pleased to hear that the last rites of his wife were performed according to Hindu rites.

"Have you told Akka about mother's death?"

"I did but..."

"But what?"

"Her memory has totally lapsed."

A few months later, Suresh was down with viral fever and when the temperature subsided he remained weak for a long time. He had lost weight. Nakul noticed wrinkles on his face and blackness around the eyes. He told his father to take care about his health.

"How old are you?"

"Sixty eight."

"That's not much of an age but if you don't take care of your health, you may succumb because of your anxieties and strain in looking after Akka. Your feelings apart, you must understand that nothing can be done to Akka and she cannot get back her years."

"What do you want me to do?"

"Spend your time in a relaxed manner. You can take a few days off for going to holiday resorts or visiting your sisters.

---

1. Priest.

You can never feel happy here with Akka in the next room. You need change. Try to understand my feelings; I have lost my mother and I don't want to lose you."

"What should we do about Akka? Someone has to look after her."

"That can be managed. You know my views. You have to face realities and agree to my practical proposition."

"OK, go ahead."

Nakul was happy. At long last his father had reconciled to the realities. He and his friend Vinay started looking for alternative place for Akka. They visited several homes for the aged. These homes did not meet their requirement for several reasons: the homes did not accept dementia patients; the expenditure involved was heavy as they would have to employ two nurses exclusively for her; their doctor saw inmates only twice in a week, for the remaining days they would have to make their own arrangements; the concept of the homes for the aged was altogether different and they were not designed for terminal cases and lastly the homes did not like gloomy atmosphere in their premises as it would affect others.

Vinay suggested that they might visit some of the hospitals. Nakul dismissed the idea; the facilities in the hospitals would not be any different and they would be much more expensive. He told his friend, "We don't have the riches of Big B."

Once while returning to the flat they saw a notice near the lift, 'One bed room flat available on rent.' Vinay exclaimed, "You got solution to your problem!" They met the flat owner. He asked rent of ₹ 3000 per month and minimum stay of one year. That was reasonable.

Suresh was happy that Akka would be lodged just a floor below. The nurses too were happy, as they would enjoy privacy. Their family doctor living in the same building would continue to look after her.

Nakul asked his father—

"How do you like the new arrangement?"

"It is good. There was always a depressing feeling with Akka in the house and that has disappeared. I now feel relaxed but very lonely. That reminds me, "When are you going to get married?"

"Very soon."

"What does that mean?"

"Next year."

Nakul after doing CA had taken up a well-paid job in a company. He was in love with a girl who was doing speciality in medicine. Suresh was aware of this relationship, had liked the girl and wanted his son to get married at an early date.

Dr. Kulkarni who was looking after Akka for the last thirty years was their family physician and a good friend.

Suresh and the doctor were talking to each other when Nakul returned from the office. Suresh went down to see his mother. That was the ideal opportunity for Nakul to talk to the doctor on an issue, which was harrowing his mind for several months. He asked-

"How is my grandmother?"

"There is no change in her condition."

"How long will she live on like this?"

"God only knows. I know that you people do not believe in God neither do I, but it is a convenient phrase for the doctors."

"What about her sufferings?"

"Her suffering is of a different type. The nurses report her condition to me every morning and evening. She cannot speak but if she gets pain she will cry and that is not happening."

"Doctor, you know her more than I do. She suffered hardships for fifteen years in bringing up her children. Well, that was a different kind of suffering. She told me years back when she was fully conscious that one should not live beyond certain age and become a burden on others. And that is precisely what is happening to her now? She has gone completely senile, she does not recognise anyone including my father and she does not speak; she is just living on."

"That is true."

"Is there any way for her to get release from this type of punishment?"

Dr. Kulkarni smiled. "I do not know what is in your mind, but if you are hinting at euthanasia, it is strictly not permissible. It is against the law and doctors cannot help in this matter."

"Actually I wanted to talk to you on this very subject. I did not know how to open the topic. Let the discussion be purely academic; would you permit me to proceed further?"

"It is OK from my side, go ahead."

"I checked up the dictionary meaning of euthanasia. It means gentle and easy death in respect of incurable and painful diseases. Now, what is wrong with that?"

"Misuse. People don't like to look after old people beyond a certain age, when their utility is zero. The term incurable and painful diseases do not necessarily apply to the aged people; such diseases can equally afflict children and young people. It can be used as a convenient tool to get rid of unwanted ones and in our country the women would be the worst sufferers. As far as medical profession is concerned, how does one know that the disease is incurable till such time all efforts have been made? Now look, the way you people are looking after Akka is admirable, but there are others who would prefer a short cut."

"Doctor, there is a truth in what you say. Amongst the poor people, they do not bother much about the old and the aged. And that happens because they don't have money to spend on them. I also know that there are people who adopt most loathsome practice of abandoning them in temples, holy places, forests and the riverbanks. Nobody says anything to them. Why does the law prevent genuine cases? Most of our laws are negative; you cannot do this and you cannot do that, there are very few laws which are positive. Gentle and easy death has a humanitarian angle!"

"You have a point but euthanasia is not permitted even in the developed countries though a lot of discussion goes on. Holland is the only country where it is legal. It would be very difficult to introduce any such law in our country. The religious leaders will oppose it tooth and nail. They believe that God has given life and we have no right to take it away."

"It is unfortunate that the religions come in the way of progress. They oppose birth control which has become a dire necessity. In due course we will be able to free ourselves from the religious shackles. But we must start thinking on this line. Misuse can be prevented by incorporating safeguards."

"I agree with you, we should. You see, everyone wants painless death but that does not happen. As a doctor, I have seen people suffering from excruciating pain from all kinds of disorders. The patients cry, shake their limbs in a violent manner and grapple for vital breath. The sight is most disgusting."

"What do you do in such cases?"

"You have asked me an awkward question but I will answer you. I give sedative to patients, tell nurses to look after them and quietly I leave the room. I do not like to see the sight of approaching death."

"I am told of certain practices in the hospitals which appear queer to me. When the condition of the patient becomes hopeless, the doctors ask the relatives of the patient if they should put him on life support for which the relatives would have to bear extra expenditure. In most cases they opt out as the amount involved is heavy, there is no certainty for survival and the end can be foreseen. The doctors play safe; they obtain written consent of relatives, dispense with expensive therapy and allow the patient to die in agony. Tell me, how moral is this practice?"

Dr. Kulkarni was quiet for a while. "Look my boy, one has to be practical. The hospitals are not charity institutions and they have to charge money. The doctors cannot pay from their pockets. The relatives do what is best under the circumstances. Here, no morality is involved. But I see your point; life is full of absurdities and we show helplessness. I must tell you that one day all of us have to die."

"We show helplessness because we have no choice but that is not a positive sign. Tell me, is there anything immoral about euthanasia?"

"It has nothing to do with morals. It is a question of social acceptance. If people want it, the laws can be framed with all possible safeguards and in that case the doctors would do the needful as a part of their professional duty. It has nothing to do with God, religion or karma."

Suresh had returned. Dr. Kulkarni left the flat saying that he had a very interesting discussion with Nakul.

There was a buzz and Geeta came in. She was the one with whom Nakul was going to get married.

Suresh asked, "Tell me if we have missed out anything in the marriage preparations?"

"Nothing that I can think of."

When Suresh left, Geeta told Nakul, "Your father is meticulous and full of enthusiasm."

"He really is and there is a reason for it. Our flat has been gloomy for a long time and you are required to bring life in it."

It was late in the night. There was a call and Nakul picked up the telephone. Vinay had rung him; his father was in a precarious condition. Nakul told him that he was leaving straightway.

Vinay had lost his mother when he was young. His father had brought him up with great care and affection. Vinay recalled the sacrifices made by his father and did everything possible to make him comfortable in his old age.

Nakul had suggested a match for his friend. She lived close by. She was liked by Vinay and his father. The engagement took place five years ago and it coincided with 85th birthday of Akka. Six months later, they got married and the three of them lived happily.

Vinay's father fell ill a year ago. He did not respond to normal medicines. When detailed investigations were carried out, it was discovered that he was suffering from blood cancer. He underwent chemotherapy and felt relieved, but that lasted only for a few months. The malady was back with greater intensity.

When Nakul reached the house, he found Vinay in tears. His friend told him that his father was in a miserable state. Nakul saw the old man lying in the bed wailing and shrieking. He was twisting his body from side to side and kicking his feet. His hands were clasped above his head and were moving up and down. He was praying to God to end his life.

Vinay said that it was becoming difficult for him to see his father in that condition and that's why he called him.

Nakul rang up Dr. Kulkarni. He came within half an hour and examined the patient. The doctor took the boys aside in the hall and told them that the old man was nearing his end. Vinay was agitated; he said, "We know that but can't you do something which will relieve him from the unbearable pain?"

The doctor glanced at Nakul recalling their recent dialogue. He told them, "Look I treat you as my children, my sincere advice to you is— don't go into that room. I will brief the nurse and she will do the needful."

Dr. Kulkarni had left. The nurse closed the door of the room. She detached the drip and other attachments. She gave sedative to the patient, placed a transistor near the pillow and inserted a cassette of *bhajans*[1]. She raised the volume loud enough for the patient to hear.

The two boys could not hold themselves for long. After sometime, they got up and quietly opened the door. They had a look at the old man; he was not crying any more, his body was still and his hands were clasped as before but they were not moving up and down. His face was calm and his eyes had

1. Devotional Song.

a few drops of tears. The transistor was close to his ears playing *bhajans.*

The nurse told them that the old man was praying and they should not disturb him. She told them to go away; she would call them if they were required. What she did not tell them was that the old man was thoroughly exhausted; he did not have strength even to move his limbs.

Nakul and Vinay sat down in the drawing room. Vinay's wife brought coffee for them. Vinay said, "To see my father in that condition was unbearable. I am glad that you came. Why can't the doctors put such patients to sleep?"

Nakul told him about his discussion with the doctor on euthanasia. "We are helpless in many matters and we have to develop acceptance. We have to go through all this and yet we must remain cheerful."

Two hours had passed. The dawn was about to break; they heard the chirruping of birds, the sign of life breaking the silence of the night. The nurse came in to announce that the old man was no more.

It was ninetieth birthday of Akka. Her sons, daughters with their spouses, grand and great grandchildren had come for the occasion. Suresh had organised the party in the similar fashion as on her eighty-fifth birthday. The get together of the family was lively and everyone enjoyed it. The only difference was that Akka could not be present even for a short while and no one wished her a long life, as they did on the previous occasion.

The guests left on the next day. Before leaving they went to see Akka. She was lying on the bed with headrest slightly raised. Her shrunken and emaciated body was naked, covered by a cloth. Her eyes were closed and mouth fully open to breathe air. They saw Akka from the door way and no one went near her. They had a brief look and departed. The young children were not allowed to see the figure of life in death and death in life.

WHERE DO THE FOLLIES END?

ASHOK AND I ARE GOOD FRIENDS from the school days. We studied together in Delhi but thereafter I had to leave the city because of my employment in Mumbai. However, despite the distance we meet frequently for one reason or the other.

I am a lawyer by profession. For the first ten years, I worked with a law company and once I got adequate experience and confidence, I started my own practice. I am not one of those biggies who mint money at the cost of their health and leisure. My needs are few and that may be because I am a bachelor. Once, an old wise man told me that it is better to be a happy bachelor than suffer the ordeals of a miserable married man. I have followed his advice.

My friend has been facing problems pertaining to his daughter and her sailor husband. He lives in Delhi and therefore he relies very heavily on me.

Ashok is a businessman. He is running the inherited family business profitably. Delhi is a place where you can sell anything and to his good luck he is in garment business. Fashion within fifty years of Independence has become a craze. Once he told me that our country has rapidly acquired consumer orientation, competing with the West. There was no need for him to tell me that; Mumbai is one up.

He married Sunita when he was just twenty-five years old. Traditionally the business community has always been eager on early marriages and in his case it was particularly so being the only child. Two years later, a daughter was born to them. Sunita faced certain gynaecological problems and she could not conceive any more. Ashok felt sad; he was looking for a male child to look after his business. As the years passed he reconciled; the situation had changed, the girls were making entry in all fields of activity. The fond parents concentrated their efforts on Kalpana.

Kalpi did her graduation in commerce. She had grown into a smart and bold girl. She understood that one day she would have to shoulder the responsibilities of her father's business. For practical experience, she joined an import and export company in Mumbai. Her father agreed to her going; he felt that it would be better if she learns finer points of business in an established company outside instead of pampered learning at home.

Kalpi had gone to the bank for drawing cash. The ATM machine was out of order and the technicians were setting it right. She was told to wait. Besides her, there was a boy in a similar predicament. They cursed the bank for inefficiency and entered into conversation to kill time. That very evening, she met the same boy in a coffee house. A beginning of friendship was made and thereafter they met each other on weekends and in between whenever possible.

Next time when Kalpana went to Dehi, she told her parents about her boy friend. Ashok said that it would be good for her if she selected someone from the business community in Delhi, which would enable them to live and work together. Kalpana said that her selection is one better; he is a sailor, he goes out for months together and that would give time to herself and the business. It is irritating to have a man around for twenty-four hours.

My friend and his wife came to Mumbai to make enquiries about the boy. Karan lives in Mahim, three local stations away from my place. His father works in Mazgaon docks. He has a son and a daughter. He had taken pains to educate his son and advised him to join shipping. Karan followed the advice and joined a shipping company as an apprentice at the age of eighteen. Karan is a smart boy. He does not smoke and drink, and is a veggie with sweet tongue.

Ashok liked the boy but he had reservations. The boy belonged to a middle class family and therefore not compatible. Sunita commented that this drawback in a way might be good for Kalpi; he won't take liberties and bully her. The parents of Karan were more than pleased to get a girl from a rich family, the sole beneficiary of parental property. Kalpi was happy to have her own way.

Ashok tallied their horoscopes; they matched. Karan and Kalpana were married in a lavish style.

The rift between Kalpi and Karan started surfacing six months after their marriage. Karan was sexy; for him every day and night on the shore mattered whereas Kalpana was content with Saturday nights. She worked from morning to evening in the office but Karan did not know what to do sitting in the house. Karan wanted his wife to conceive while she was firmly against it for several more years. Three months later Karan went to the sea and Kalpi felt relieved.

1990 was the year of glut in shipping. A large number of sailors and seamen were sitting idle waiting for their turn in the long queue. Karan's stay in Mumbai was unusually long. They were also the days when his father was not keeping well. He was shuttling between Mahim and his wife's posh flat in Colaba.

The condition of his father became serious. The old man felt that it was time for him to make a WILL. Karan told his father that the house and other assets should be bequeathed to him and he would look after his mother and sister. It would keep the family together and not dissipate the property. The old man agreed.

Karan's unemployment and the sickness of his father were causing expenditure beyond his means. He wrote to his father in-law for help. Ashok was generous; he sent him double the amount asked for.

The glut in the shipping was over and Karan managed to get a job. This time he decided to remain on sea for a long period. However, after two months his father expired and he returned to Mumbai. He could not be present for the cremation but he managed to reach for *Shradha*[1] ceremony. He asked his father in-law to send some more money because of bereavement and the requirement for him to remain on shore till the family problems were sorted out. My friend complied.

I had gone to Delhi. All my relatives are there and it is normal for me to make two to three trips every year. Ashok and Sunita were keen to know about their son in-law. I told them that the last time when I met him he was furious.

"What happened?" Sunita asked.

A fortnight after the death of the old man, I was called upon to open the Will. It read that all assets and property were bequeathed equally to his survivors namely his wife, son and daughter and he nominated Karan as executor.

"A very sensible Will," my friend commented.

"Yup," but Karan did not like it. He wanted to be the sole inheritor. He said that he had told his father to bequeath the entire property to him and he in turn would look after his mother and sister. His father had agreed. But this Will was worded differently. He exclaimed, "I do not know who prevailed upon my father to make such a Will!"

"Not me," I said.

"Who has the first right on the property?" He asked in anger.

---

1. The last ritual of the mourning period.

"Your mother." I explained to him that the Will was in order, acceptable in the courts of law. All Wills are subject to litigation and a Will is not an authority for implementation. There are a large number of cases under litigation in the courts because of faulty Wills.

Karan was fuming. "It is all shit," he said and left. A fortnight later he was back on the sea.

Ashok and Sunita had come to Mumbai to spend a few days with their daughter. Kalpi was happy, happy because her husband was on the sea and she could spend all the time with her parents.

"What's the latest?" Ashok enquired.

Karan's mother came to see me. He had employed an agent for transfer of Mahim flat in his name. Before proceeding on the sea, he had submitted an application to the corporation stating that he has been appointed as executor; he intends to sell the flat and thereafter disburse the proceeds equally to the three survivors.

She asked me if this could be done. I told her that it is possible if it is not challenged. People bribe the corporation staff and get the work done according to their wishes. All that the corporation does is to put a notice on the board, wait for the stipulated period and if there is no objection, they implement it.

The poor lady was in tears. She confided to me that her son, despite his apparent good qualities, suffers from some serious drawbacks. He is very authoritative and has weakness for money. He does not listen and can be cruel.

I asked her what she wants me to do. She said that the flat must not be sold; if that is done, she will have no place to live, and she will be thrown out on the street. She has to live somewhere and has a daughter to look after.

I assured her that this can be done. She will have to contest and file an application.

Sunita asked me, "Where does the case stand?"

I have filed the case. It will take donkey's years to sort out and until then they can live on in the same flat.

Kalpi said that her mother in-law had become very friendly with her ever since this incident. She had smelt right from the beginning that he cannot be trusted with money. She complained, "Papa, you have been sending him money without asking me!"

Ashok said, "Look, I want harmonious relationship. The money that I have given him was a trifle."

Kalpi retorted, "He gets enough money, which is tax free. He has never spent a pie on me or the house!"

Sunita looked towards me. "We must find out where does he spend his money?" I said, "It would be worthwhile doing that."

Ashok and I were having a drink. We do that in the evenings strictly adhering to the limits laid down by the doctors.

He said, "It is a strange case. I do not know what my son in-law is up to. Think of it, he does not drink, does not smoke and is a veggie."

I told him that such men could be dangerous. They have no outlet to let off the steam. They keep on thinking, mulling, build up pressure, pile up anger and finally do something stupid.

Ashok agreed. "In our daily life we experience hurdles, obstructions and irritants but we get over them by the evening and start afresh the next morning."

"The trouble with Karan is that he has no hobbies. He does not go for jog in the mornings or play any game."

"That is true," said my friend. "He has caused me pain but what he is doing to his mother and sister is worse. Why did he want to sell the flat? Is he all that hard up for money? That reminds me, you remember what Sunita had said? We must find out where does he spend his money?"

I told him that it would not be difficult. There are many

private detective agencies in the city and I will hire one of them. They will keep a track on him when he returns. I told Ashok that we should focus our attention on Kalpi; she should remain cool.

"Oh Kalpi, she is quite cool and composed. You know, this generation is so different from us. They are not bothered if marriages are broken; their priorities are different. It is me who gets worried. I can only hope that all ends well."

Karan was back. He first went to his flat in Mahim. He sensed discomfiture; it was not the same feeling of warmth with his mother and sister. Soon he learnt from the agent that the property could not be transferred in his name. His mother had filed a case and it was admitted in the civil court for hearing. The first date for hearing was fixed after two years.

He went to his wife's flat. Kalpana was cold. She told him that a crack had appeared in their relationship and it might not get resolved. Karan understood his predicament; he was not welcome in both the places and he must make an alternative arrangement.

Meanwhile the detective agency was at work. They trailed Karan for two weeks. They reported that during daytime, he visits a smallish dwelling in Girgaon. The residents are an old man who has lost vision from both the eyes and a lusty girl who works as waitress in a restaurant during evening shifts. Karan and the girl are very friendly and spend hours together every day.

The report had only given a clue. I was not satisfied. I wanted details. The agency asked for 5000/- for the job already done and 20000/- as advance to probe for more information. I paid them the amount. I had no choice; that is how this business works, first they throw bait and then grab!

After another two weeks, a man from the detective agency came to meet me. He revealed the name of the girl as Latika; she works in Ayesha restaurant. She is a lusty, dusky girl around

25 years and has good features. He showed me a photograph of the girl and then took it back.

"For how long has Karan been visiting that place?"

"Almost a year."

"Do other men frequent that place?"

"No."

"What is their relationship like?"

"They are intimate. It started with an incident outside the restaurant. Two men sufficiently tipsy tried to drag the girl in their car at the closing time. Karan intervened and dropped Latika to her residence."

"Does she know that Karan is a married man?"

"Yes. Karan tells her everything. He told her that his wife is frigid and haughty. His marriage is on the verge of break up. Her parents wanted a son in-law who would remain in the house and work according to their bidding. He was roped in because of their wealth. His parents made a big blunder and ruined his matrimonial life. His mother still wants him to continue with his wife but that is not possible. He is at a loss. He is home loving and wants a respectable life but he is not getting it. He told Latika that he would like to marry her. His earnings are adequate to lead a comfortable life but he must acquire a decent place to live. That needs money; he has already saved a lot of money but that is not enough for a flat in Mumbai. During his last meeting, he told her that he has got a very lucrative offer in a company. It involves risk but he is going to take it as a challenge. He would be back after six months and by then his monetary problems should be over."

"What was the reaction of that girl to Karan's proposal?"

"She is willing to marry him and is waiting for his return."

"How did you get this information?"

"We made use of a girl who works in the same restaurant. She claims to be her friend. We had to spend ₹ 5000 on her."

"How authentic is your information?"

"We have done the cross check. Now it is up to you. We

don't give anything in writing and we do not act as witness."

The information that I got fitted in the overall picture. The man asked me if I had any other service for him. I said, "No, thank you." I had to pay him ₹ 10,000 more.

I rang up Ashok in Delhi. The situation had taken an ugly turn after the disclosure by the detective agency. He said that he would reach Mumbai next morning.

I am waiting for Ashok and Sunita. The flight is two hours late but that would not matter. Kalpana had rung up, she had got stuck in the office but she said that she would positively reach by lunchtime.

Today we have to take a harsh decision. I am recollecting the events that have been going on for the last two and a half years. I feel sorry for my friend, his wife and daughter.

When Ashok and Sunita came I told them details of investigation. Sunita said that Kalpi would not tolerate him any more. She upbraided her husband for being soft to Karan and sending him money. Ashok admitted his mistake and told me to file divorce proceedings. He added that Kalpi had finished her assignment in Mumbai and he would take her back to Delhi. For him it was an unpleasant *Salaam*[1] to Mumbai.

Kalpi came in a terrible angry mood. She said that her jewellery box was missing. That cheat, Karan must have stolen. I can well visualize the reason; he needed money to buy a flat.

It was a sad day. We did not talk much. Ashok's all hopes were shattered. They departed after lunch. Two days later they boarded a plane and Kalpi left Mumbai for good.

Sometime later Karan's mother came to meet me. She was in tears. She told me that her son had been brutally killed.

"What happened," I asked.

A day before, she got a call from the police station located near the fishermen's colony at Mahim. She was told to collect

1. Farewell.

the dead body of her son. She along with her daughter scrambled to the police station. There she was told that the fishermen had found a dead body floating on the sea. A laminated card was affixed to the body notifying name and address. When the face was uncovered, she identified her son.

"Did the police give you any details about the horrid incident?"

She shook her head in the negative. The police told her that they were trying to ascertain details but that would take time. Meanwhile she could file a written complaint. She did that, brought the dead body to the house and cremated him. She handed me a laminated card; written on it was name, address and diabolical message- Wish you a better luck in the next birth.

She started crying. She said that it was a cold-blooded murder. She asked me if I could help her.

I promised her that I would do my best.

After two days a good-looking dusky girl with sharp features knocked on my door. She introduced herself as Latika. She showed me a laminated card similar to one which Karan's mother had received. She asked me if Karan was dead.

I related to her the details which had transpired between me and Karan's mother.

Latika was in tears. She said, "It is all over for me, I lived in a dream world for one year." She pulled out a kerchief, wiped her tears and gained composure. She took out a jewellery box from the satchel hung round her shoulder and placed it on the table. "This belongs to Kalpana. Can you send it across to her?"

I told her that it would be done. Kalpana had reported the loss to me. I was going to the police station to file a case against Karan. You came just in time. I opened the box; it contained most sophisticated and expensive jewellery of gold and diamonds.

"How did you get my address?"

"Karan had been talking to me about you."

I thanked her about her honesty. I told her that other girls in similar situation would have pocketed the entire fortune.

There was a sordid smile on her face. She said, "Look, I am a poor girl. If I sell the jewellery I would be questioned and get caught. If I employ a middleman he will take full advantage and I will get nothing. If I wear that jewellery the police would apprehend me for stolen property. The best course for me is to return the jewellery to its owner and be out of it."

I was stunned by the simple, straightforward and practical sense of the girl. I spoke to Ashok. He told me to compensate the girl.

I told Latika, "My friend is very grateful to you. He has asked me to give you ₹ 1 lakh as reward.

Latika smiled. "I am a poor girl burdened with responsibility to look after my father. Money will help me but I don't want to get into greed and another set of trouble. Don't you know what has happened to Karan? You can leave me alone; I am perfectly satisfied with my lot."

I assured her that she would not get into any trouble. I told her that I am a lawyer; giving gift is legal and she would get a signed letter along with the cheque.

Before leaving, Latika gave me a file containing miscellaneous papers of Karan, details of his bank accounts, appointment letters from the shipping company etc.

My next task has been made easy. The file contains details of Karan's employer. Goldline Shipping Co has its office opposite to Indira docks in Colaba.

They are very decent and polite people. Their officer welcomed me and made me comfortable with a cup of coffee. When I told him about the purpose of my visit, he opened the computer and was ready to answer all my questions.

"Karan Singh joined us on 25th of July and was assigned to ship JAL TARANG as Chief Officer. The ship was employed for carriage of cargo, to and fro, between Middle East and various ports on our western coast. On first of November, the ship was to sail from Dubai and Karan did not report back at the stipulated time for duty. We informed the police and employed another officer. We do not have any knowledge of Mr Karan Singh thereafter."

"How do you know that Karan was not on the ship?"

The officer smiled. "We maintain a manifest of cargo and crew list. It is a mandatory requirement."

"Karan's dead body was found 20 kms away from Mahim in the open sea. How did that happen?"

"How would we know that? It is for the police at Dubai and Mumbai to carry out investigation."

"How was the behaviour and conduct of Karan Singh on board the ship?"

He pressed few buttons and said, "Satisfactory. Nothing adverse has been reported."

The officer asked me a question. "When was dead body of Mr Karan Singh found?"

"It was found on 25th November. The death might have occurred a day or two earlier."

"Let me see," he said. He pressed a few buttons, "Ah, here it is. The ship on that day was in Dubai, nowhere near Mumbai."

My visit to Goldline Co was no good. I did not get any clue. I must find out details from the police about the mysterious death.

The visit to police headquarters was annoying; for one, there was a big crowd of visitors and then I was shunted from one desk to the other, and finally when I reached the correct place, I was told that the officer is not present. I had to wait for two hours.

When he came he seemed to be in a great hurry. I told him about Karan, his ghastly murder and dead body thrown into the sea. He did not appear to take much interest. He said that they would try to find out but the chances were dim.

I told him that Karan is son in-law of a prominent businessman and I am his lawyer.

"That may be so, but as far as this murder is concerned it is the work of mafia and they don't leave behind any clues. The people involved are shipping companies, the agents who receive and despatch cargo and mafia who superimpose themselves upon them. Mafia make use of ships for contraband, which is a very lucrative business. They are very particular about secrecy and loyalty. They pay well but any act of indiscipline meets with death penalty. They publicise it as warning to others. Karan must have done something which has offended them."

"The shipping company told me that the ship was nowhere near Mumbai when he was murdered."

The officer smiled. He told me to read some books on mafia and their way of working. Surely they will not commit murder and send the dead body on the listed ship. They are professional and they have been in the game for a long, long time.

He got up to go on urgent call. As he was going, he said that the police and coast guard were always on the lookout for the criminals but unfortunately the rate of success was not very encouraging.

Sometime later I went to Delhi. It was a breezy month of December. We were sitting in the balcony basking in the pleasant sun. I asked my friend about Kalpi.

"Oh, Kalpi," he said, "she is fine; she does not feel sad and has no regrets. It is I who worries. I have to find a suitable match for her."

"Yes, you must do that," I said. "Do you have anyone in mind?"

"There are two boys, but this time I am going to be very careful."

I smiled and told him to take care. I told him about the

mysterious death of Karan. He was killed by mafia leaving no evidence behind. No one knows why. Apparently he was trying to be clever with them wanting more money. "But I tell you that the girl, Latika is very sensible; I was impressed by her down to earth, straight behaviour."

"Do you think that Karan would have married that girl?

"It is a difficult question to answer but he did make use of her to satisfy his lust and the custody of stolen jewellery."

"Do these boys realize where such follies lead to?"

A funeral procession was passing by on the street. We stood up as a mark of respect for the departed soul when the procession approached the house.

RAM NAM SATYA·HAI[1]

1. A phrase which people chant during funeral procession, 'The name of Ram is truth'.

MAMATA

MAMATA CHATTERJEE had finished the day's work and was looking forward to an enjoyable week end. She rang up her friend and told her that she intended to visit her place. Sharmila was delighted.

"I am glad that you have decided to come. You have been promising me for a long time. Tell me, how do you want to spend your break?"

"I leave that to you."

"OK. I will work out the details to suit your taste, but you also give a thought. Luckily I am free with all my time for you."

The sun was down by the time, Mamata reached her apartment. She had a quick wash, packed her clothes and was off in a vibrant mood. For the last few weeks she had been working overtime drawing on her reserve energy. As a doctor she could not neglect the patients and in a country like America she had to be careful lest she got involved in medico-legal cases. She stopped 20 kms away from her apartment to fill gas.

A cop came to her car at the refuelling station.

"You a doctor?"

"Yup."

"Get down; there is an urgent case for you."

Mamata was taken, a little distance away, to a car parked on the periphery of the gas station. There, she saw two old women apparently unconscious. She examined them; their pulse and blood pressure was low.

"Do they have a driver?"

"No."

"They need hospitalisation."

"Do that," said the Cop.

Mamata rang up her hospital for ambulance. She rang up her friend and told her about the unfortunate incident. Her plan for the week-end was thrown off.

When the ambulance came, the two women were checked up once again and taken to the hospital. They were taken to the intensive care unit and put on drip. Mamata was attending to them.

The police traced the identity of the two women from the number plate of the car and handed over the details to Mamata. She dialled a number. It was attended by Alex Hilton.

"I am Doctor Mamata Chatterjee speaking from Columbus hospital, Ohio. Your mother is admitted in our hospital, her condition is serious and we are trying to revive her. You are advised to look her up."

"That is not possible at this time of the night. Tomorrow I am busy. The earliest that I can visit her would be on Monday. Keep me informed."

Mamata rang up the kith of the other lady. It was picked up by her daughter, Caroline. "I feel so sad to hear that. I spoke to mom this morning, she was fine. Now look, I am speaking from a beach resort. It is a long drive from Ohio and it would take me eight hours to reach. I am spending my week-end here with my children. I am going to be back on Monday, until then please look after her. Let me know if her condition deteriorates further."

Mamata was not happy with their response. She contended herself in the thought that she had done her duty.

The two women remained critical for several hours. By morning there was a perceptible change in their condition and they had regained consciousness. On Sunday they were kept under observation and by Monday morning they were out of danger. Alex and Caroline did not turn up; they did not see any necessity.

The ladies were in late seventies and friends. They were widows placed in the similar plight of living alone. They were neighbours and got along extremely well. They had decided to spend the week end in a farm house and were on their way. When they were nearing the gas station, they felt giddy with intense pain in the stomach and chest region. Somehow, they managed to reach the gas station and there they fainted. They could not comprehend the reason; it could have been due to extra pegs of vodka, fish or something else. The material thing was that both of them got attack at the same time. They were lucky to get hold of a cop at the refuelling station.

They stayed in the hospital for two more days and were discharged in a fit condition. They felt sad that their children did not turn up in the hospital to see them but that was not something unusual in America, where everyone remains involved in their own affairs and have no time for others.

Financially they were well to do. They paid the cheque and gave generous presents to Mamata. They expressed their gratitude to her and apologised for spoiling her week end. They invited her to their houses, which were close by. Mamata did that. She became their personal physician and visited them regularly.

Mamata had gone to US four years ago. She had graduated in medicine from Kolkata and had gone to America out of frustration. In four year's time she had established herself and gained a good reputation. She was comfortable living in a good apartment with steady income and all amenities. What she liked most was freedom, which she never got in India. She could move about, mix freely and enjoy parties.

Was she happy? Not really. She missed Bangla and that was not something confined to language. It was a totality of environment in which she was born and brought up; of language, food, customs, music, dance, festivals and relatives. She missed her parents, brothers, sisters, uncles, aunts and cousins. It was a world of its own to keep her occupied. In India she was involved, in US she felt lonely in the flat with no one around. But more than any other thing she missed her boyfriend.

During the college days, Mamata had fallen in love with a Malayali boy. His father had served for many years in Kolkata as accountant in a company. After retirement, he had gone back to his village near Thiruvanthapuram leaving behind his son to complete his education. Raghavan Nambudri was staying in the college hostel.

Once during recess hour for lunch, an accident took place between a taxi and a rickshaw near the entrance gate of the college. Raghavan and Mamata happened to be nearby. They rushed to the scene; a middle aged man and a woman travelling in the rickshaw were seriously injured. The two students with the help of others carried the injured to the Casualty Wing of the hospital for treatment. The couple had fractured their limbs and the blood was oozing out. They were attended to by the surgeons, operated upon and transferred to the ward. The two students met the patients in the mornings and evenings and that had become a regular feature for them till such time that the patients were discharged from the hospital. That was the beginning of their liking for each other. The stir in their heart had taken place and they continued to meet each other at different venues like the college library, the lawns and the banyan tree. At the end of two years when they were in the final year, they realised that they were in love and expressed their desire to get married.

The feelings apart, both of them knew that they would face problem in their marriage. They belonged to different community and regions far away from each other. Mamata's father was most vocal; he detested the idea of his daughter marrying anyone other than a Bengali. Mamata pleaded that though the boy was from South India, their family had lived for a long time in Kolkata. Her boyfriend was born and brought up in the city and spoke fluent Bengali.

"That does not make him a Bengali!"

"I want to tell you that he is a Brahmin."

"That makes no difference."

"Baba, I have known him for four years. He is well behaved and the family is cultured. Marriages involve risk; how can I marry a boy whom I do not know and love?"

"That's the trouble with girls of present days. Love! What does that mean? Such ideas had never struck us. This is final from my side; you will marry a Bengali and no one else."

"If that's the condition I will never marry."

The situation was different with Raghavan Nambudri. His father had written a long letter. He had cautioned his son about the problem of adjustment when the boy and the girl belong to a different cultural milieu. Marriages involve interaction between the families; it is not restricted to husband and wife. Adjustment is a genuine problem for grown up people and in this case both of them are doctors with set minds. However, the most important aspect is compatibility; the boy and the girl temperamentally must get along, resolved to go through good and bad times.

"I have not met the girl and her family. I do not know what to say. I went to our family astrologer with your horoscope. He said that you will enjoy a very happy married life but the marriage is not likely to take place before five to six years. You have just graduated and are too young to get married. The astrologer said that you would face hurdles but ultimately you would marry the girl of your choice.

I believe in horoscopes. The previous predictions in your case have been true. I therefore leave the decision to you. All that I would advise you is caution, don't be in a hurry."

Mamata and Raghavan talked to each other regarding the views of their parents. Mamata said that she liked the views expressed by his father. He was conservative but not dogmatic like her father.

Raghavan said, "He has left it to me. You see, he has lived his life outside Kerala and therefore he has an open mind. Your father has never moved out of Bengal and therefore he is rigid. To me, the views of our Guruji are important. We revere him; whatever he says turns out to be right. He had predicted that I will take medicine as my career and that has been true. Sometimes, I do believe in supernatural. The situation is not hopeless. The Guruji has assured that I will marry the girl of my choice. What more can I wish? We have yet to establish ourselves and therefore we can wait. I don't understand one aspect; Guruji has said that I will face hurdles. What hurdles, I do not know?"

"My father obviously," said Mamata.

Raghavan smiled. "That it is but it will get sorted out in due course if you are firm. Our immediate concern should be, what are we going to do now?"

"I have decided to go abroad," said Mamata. "I have told my father that if I don't marry you, I will not marry anyone else."

Mamata had a great fascination for Durga Puja. She revered the deity. She went to US soon after Puja. She was resolved that her stay in America was going to be temporary. She must earn and save money as that would give her freedom of action. Her final objective was to marry her boyfriend and settle down in Kolkata. She started counting her stay in US from Durga Puja. She managed a temporary job in a hospital at Ohio. Her performance was good and after two years of hard work, she got the reward, a permanent employment.

Raghavan did internship in the same college and got a job there only after one year. Simultaneously he started studies for speciality in surgery.

Mamata and Raghavan spoke to each other every week and sometimes they wrote long letters. Her boyfriend told her to remain cool; the path of true love never runs along a straight line.

Mamata visited her home after completion of two years, her first homecoming after going to US. She could manage to get only three weeks off but that was good enough. She had planned her holidays during Durga Puja and enjoyed her stay in Kolkata. She was making up for all that she had missed in America i.e. music, dance and theatre; she enjoyed Bengali meals of *hilsa*[1], rice, *mishti dahi*[2] and sweets. Meeting her relatives and friends was a great fun.

Her evenings were spent with Raghavan. Once when they had gone out for shopping to Hati Bagan, they were caught in the rains. They took shelter in the nearby *pandal*[3] erected for Puja. They bought flowers and garlands and slowly walked up to the idol. The priest mistook them as newly married couple and blessed them for a happy married life. They looked at each other in amazement and smiled. Mamata out of zest placed her garland round Raghavan's neck and so did he.

When the showers eased they went to Raghavan's flat. Mamata removed her wet sari and spread it under the fan to dry up. Raghavan changed his clothes. The blessings of the priest were fresh in their minds; he was feeling sexy and she was all worked up inside. They embraced, kissed and fondled each other for a long time and finally let themselves loose. That was their first experience opening the gate for many more.

Mamata for the remaining period of her holidays was

---

1. A variety of popular fish in Bengal.
2. Sweet curd, a delicacy in Bengal.
3. A canvas structure erected for Puja.

spending greater part of her time with Raghavan. They were treating each other like husband and wife, and she started calling him as Raghu. Her prolonged absence and late nights were noticed by the parents, and were resented by her father. Mamata too was aware of what she was doing but she did not bother and kept mum. A few days before her departure, her mother broke the silence.

"It is time that you get married. Your father has two boys in his mind. They are from good families and have permanent jobs, here itself. I have also liked them and the horoscopes are matching. Here are their photographs. Have a look."

Mamata did not show any interest. "Ma, I have already told Baba that I am not going to marry anyone else."

"Look, both of you are unnecessarily rigid. Your father is not going to change his stand and therefore you should reconcile. There is sense in what your father says; ultimately you have to stay here in Kolkata. You know it well that you don't like US, living alone by yourself. How long would you continue like this?"

Mamata quietly said that there was no point in discussion and walked out of the room.

Mamata had returned to Ohio and her third year in US had begun on happy note. She had enjoyed her communion with Raghavan; it was something which she wanted to do but was held back because her fiancé was shy. The blessing of the priest had ignited the cooped up desire and she found complete satisfaction in sexual relationship. Marriages are often wrecked because of sexual incompatibility and now that it had happened, there was nothing for her to fear. She thanked God as it fortified her choice. The fortnight of love making had left a memory and a yearning for her fiancé. She had ignored her parents and firmly said no to their proposal. After this affair, she was convinced that she was right in her resolve to marry Raghu.

The life otherwise for her was going on in the normal

manner. She remained occupied with her work and at times visited the two old women. Twice she was able to meet her friend Sharmila.

She was eagerly looking forward to vacation during Puja days. That year she could get only two weeks off and she had to contend with it. Whatever few days she got with her fiancé were bliss.

There was no change in the attitude of her father. He resented her being absent from the house for long hours. He gave vent to his anger before his wife. "Tell that girl to show restraint, she is not in America." His wife heard him and agreed with his views. Nonetheless she gave enough hints to imply that the girl is grown up and a doctor by profession.

Before her departure, Mamata's mother ventured to open the topic regarding her marriage. This time Mamata laughed. She told her mother to convey to Baba that he should stop looking for grooms; it would be a waste of time.

The fourth year for Mamata was rewarding and fruitful. It had begun with substantial raise in her salary. That meant additional savings and she needed that. She was saving money to buy a spacious flat in Kolkata, in which she and her husband could settle down comfortably after marriage. The existing flat of Raghavan on the College Street was too small. A doctor husband and wife is a good combination; they earn good money more than their requirement, remain engrossed in their activities and their busy schedule keeps them away from all mischief, extramarital or any other.

Raghavan had got the degree of MS in surgery and because of his reputation was offered a job in the same college. Before taking up the new assignment, he took two months leave. He spent a fortnight with his parents and boarded a flight from Thiruvanthapuram to America.

Mamata was thrilled. Raghavan's visit was an unexpected bonus and she made the best use of it. In that country nobody bothered about them and they behaved free from all restraints. Mamata told him that she intended to take a fortnight off. That would enable them to go to various places for sightseeing. Raghavan told her not to do that; she should preserve her off days for Durga Puja vacations.

"How will you spend your time in the flat when I go to the hospital?"

"I can read, do up the house and do shopping."

"That doesn't take much time and I know your restless nature."

"May be I could go to your hospital, meet people and if possible give a helping hand."

In no time, he became a very popular figure in Columbus hospital. The surgical staff admired his deft fingers, calm composure, polite talks and skill in surgery. There is generally an overload on surgeons and his presence gave them a respite. He too learnt a great deal about the latest equipment and technique. He was given a warm farewell party before his departure and an open invitation to join them.

Three months later, Mamata went to Kolkata. This time she got four weeks of holidays. Mamata was surprised to see warmth in the behaviour of her father. She learnt the reason from her mother.

Her father had slipped in the toilet injuring his hips and spine. He was admitted in the hospital. The x-ray and MRI revealed fracture in the hip bone and lesion injury in lower vertebrae. He had to spend a month in the hospital. He was attended to by a competent doctor with good bedside manners. The doctor visited him twice, in the morning and evening, and spoke in cultured, fluent Bengali. He appeared to be from *Bhadralok*[1]. Later on, Mr Sunil Chatterjee learnt that the doctor attending to him was not a Bengali. He was a Malayali boy whom his daughter loved.

Her mother said, "I had been telling your Baba to change

1. Class of elite, gentry.

his old, prejudiced ideas, but he would not listen. I told him that the times have changed; inter-religion, inter-caste and inter-community marriages have become a common occurrence and the young people should be allowed to have their way. The hospital incident made an impact on his mind. Now he is agreeable to marriage with your boyfriend. There is a saying in Sanskrit '*Pratyaksha Pramanam*[1]' and that has worked. But there is something which I do not like. You return from his apartment late in the night. It makes me apprehensive."

In the adjoining room, Mamata's father was listening to the conversation between the mother and daughter. He came out and butted in—

"Your mother is right. Kolkata is no longer a safe place in the nights. The hooligans, miscreants, Maoists and Naxals have become active. It would be better if you stay the night there only."

Mamata was astonished to hear that from her father. She was overwhelmed with joy. She decided to spend the night in Raghavan's flat. With big smile on her face, she told him that all hurdles are over and they could get married at any time. Raghavan told her that he had received a letter that very morning from his father. The Guruji had said, "I will get married in a year's time. There was a note of caution; I will face problems, difficulties and hurdles. However, nothing would happen to me. I have been warned to be careful."

"What hurdles and difficulties Guruji is talking about? They are over this morning."

"That part is from your side. You got the clearance. I have to watch out my side."

"Do you mean that your parents will create any problems?"

"None, whatsoever."

"Then, what is it?"

"I don't know. But it doesn't matter; the Guruji has said that nothing would happen to me. I have been advised to be

---

1. Visible evidence is proof.

careful and that I will."

Mamata had spent a happy month in Kolkata. Before her departure, her mother asked, "When are you going to get married?"

Mamata told her mother about the exchange of garland before Goddess Durga. Formal marriage was left and that should take place within year's time. Her next visit would be for marriage. This disclosure made her parents most happy.

It was normal for Raghavan to see her off. This time her parents were also present at the Netaji Subhash Chandra Bose International Airport to wish her happy journey.

The first few months of the fifth year for Mamata had passed happily. The fond memories of her last year kept lingering on in her mind. She was dreaming and planning various details of her forthcoming marriage. She thought of the dress that she would wear for the wedding, the ornaments that she would adorn, the friends whom she would call etc, etc. The regular calls from her fiancé and home kept her cheerful.

She asked Raghu if he would be able to come to US during summer vacations. He told her that he had been detailed for a surgical camp in a rural area and that would last till June. He would be able to go to US for three or four weeks in July. It was towards the end of June; Mamata rang up her boy, there was no response. She tried it repeatedly for two more days; there was no answer. She got terribly upset and rang up her parents.

Sunil Chatterjee too did not get any response from the landline or mobile number. He went to the flat of Raghavan. It was locked. He went to the medical college and met the principal. The latter told him that they were in a similar state of anxiety; Mr Raghavan Nambudri had not come to the college for the last two days. They had made enquiries from the neighbours; they had no knowledge. The only thing that they had found was a note on the door latch. It read, 'I am going out with some urgent and important work. I will be back.'

Mr Chatterjee went to the police station and lodged the complaint. He gave them the hand written note left behind by Raghavan. He urged the police to take prompt action in tracing the doctor. They showed utmost sympathy but said that they would have to wait for more clues. He rang up her daughter and informed her regarding the mysterious absence of her fiancé.

Mamata was shocked. In their last conversation, Raghavan had told her that he had returned from the camp and was going to board the flight for US. Where did he disappear suddenly? Instantly she recalled the prediction of Guruji. She called Raghu's father and asked him about the whereabouts of his son. He was not aware of anything. She told him about his disappearance and the small note left on the door. She would be going to Kolkata very soon to ascertain details.

Mr. Vijayan Nambudri was a cool headed person, one of those who do not get perturbed easily and that was due to his faith in Guruji. He told Mamata to wait for a day or two; his astrologer had foreseen certain problems and therefore he would like to consult him. Mamata said that she was aware of Guruji's prediction, but what kind of hurdle was this? Surely, he could have given details like where he was going, the nature of urgency, contact number and address! He has gone leaving everyone in dark and confused state.

Raghavan's father told Mamata to cool down. He understood her predicament and assured her that he would contact her as soon as possible. That was the first time that he had talked to her.

Vijayan rushed to meet his Guruji. The latter went through the *kundali*[1] once again and reiterated that his son would face problems but he would go through them. Vijayan had specific questions to ask. Was there any danger to his life? "No," the Guruji said assertively. The old man told Guruji about his son's love affair with a Bengali girl. Would that fructify? The Guruji

1. Horoscope.

said that he would not be able to comment till such time he examines her horoscope.

The old man rang up Mamata the next morning. He told her about his talks with Guruji and the categorical statement that there was no danger to Raghavan's life.

"That part is OK but I possibly cannot be in peace till such time he returns or we know some factual details about him. I must go to Kolkata."

"You can do that but how would that help you? You would go to the police and they would investigate details from the college, neighbours, your parents and me. They are doing that; last evening they came to me for enquiry. Now look I am his father, I am as much concerned as you are and I am doing my best. I would advise you to wait for some more time."

"I see your point Sir, but I am feeling miserable. I do not know what to do. That short note has created dreadful anxiety."

"That's true but it is better than nothing, otherwise we would be probing in total darkness, thinking of all sorts of eventualities such as murder, accidental death etc. The note has left behind a ray of hope. I am sure he will write again at the earliest opportunity."

"I do not know how to tell you my plight. I love him and we planned to get married this year."

"I am aware of that. My son had written to me. Incidentally, I had mentioned this point to Guruji. He says that he cannot comment on marriage till such time he sees your horoscope."

"That is not difficult. I will speak to my father and he will send it across to you."

The sudden disappearance of Raghavan had brought Mamata, her and his parents together. They kept on calling each other exchanging, discussing and waiting for further information. Sunil Chatterjee mailed Mamata's horoscope to Thiruvanthapuram.

Raghavan Nambudri was abducted from his flat in the dead

of the night by the Naxals. He was not allowed to communicate with anyone and was permitted to leave behind just two lines. He was driven in a van at crash speed. In the morning he reached a camp site in a wooded area. He was taken to a rural dispensary and told to remove two bullets lodged in the thigh of a patient. The operation was performed under local anaesthesia without the presence of anaesthetist. It was successful and no infection took place.

A few days later, Raghavan came to know that the person whom he had operated upon was the dreaded Naxal leader, Bhanu Biswas. He carried a cash reward of Rs. 10 lakhs on his head and therefore could not be taken to any hospital. The operation had to be carried out in a remote place. Fortunately for the patient the Naxals had picked up the right doctor.

Bhanu was recovering and the pain had started decreasing. Raghavan was attending to him every day for the change of dressing. Bhanu liked his pleasant manners and thanked him for the operation. He asked him if he was comfortable and being looked after.

"Is there anything that I can do for you?"

Raghavan said, "I was kidnapped in a hurry and brought to this place. I now understand the reason for it; you had no option other than getting a surgeon to this place. I do not mind living in forest under difficult conditions. As per medical ethics I must treat patients even if they belong to the enemy camp. My problem is that my family and friends have been left in the lurch, in the state of anxiety. They would not know if I am alive or dead. I want to write to them and assure them that I am in good health."

The Naxal leader said, "That can be done. Your letters will be despatched promptly but you must not disclose where you are. It must not contain any details regarding our camps, activities and people. Your letters will be censored."

Two weeks after the painful incident, Sunil Chatterjee received a letter. It was from Raghavan. He told his wife that they have received news from the boy; he is hale and hearty. They rang up their daughter and read out the letter to her. Mamata was delighted to get the news.

"Baba, where is he?"

"He hasn't mentioned that."

"I want to speak to him. Has he given new contact number or address?"

"No."

"That is strange. Anyway, at least we know that he is well and being looked after. Has he written a letter to his father?"

"I will speak to Mr Nambudri and find out."

Sunil Chatterjee went to the police station and met the officer who was handling the case. He read the letter, examined the envelope and smiled.

"Does this letter give you any clue regarding his whereabouts?"

"Yes, it tells everything. The envelope bears the stamp of local post office."

"Does it mean that he is in Kolkata?"

The police officer laughed at the naivety of Mr Chatterjee. He told the complainant that the doctor has been abducted by the Naxalites and taken to their camp for the treatment of their sick and wounded. This is their standard practice. They look after the doctors and release them when their work is over.

"Is there a threat to his life?"

"We have not received any such report."

"What are you going to do?"

"I am going to send this letter to our headquarters, but I want to tell you that combating with Naxals is not in our charter of responsibility."

Bhanu Biswas was an educated young man, a graduate in political science from the Presidency College, Kolkata. He was inspired by the communist ideology and took interest in the

Naxal movement right from the college days and joined their ranks soon after his education. He was fiery by temperament and took part in several raids. His best performance was in the raids on police posts at Lalgarh in May 2009. The Naxals were successful in creating a liberated zone. It was later in one of the subsequent raids that he was wounded by bullets. The Naxals admired his bravery and acknowledged his leadership.

After the operation, his condition was improving and the pain was coming down. He was brash and talkative by nature and looked forward to someone with whom he could talk freely. He liked Raghavan and looked forward to his daily visit for the change of dressing. Raghavan was a good listener and polished in his behaviour.

"You see, more than sixty years have passed since our Independence and we have done nothing to ameliorate poverty. You are now living with us and you can see what the conditions here are like. Don't you think that these people deserve better treatment?"

Raghavan shook his head up and down in the affirmative.

"People say that the poverty in our country is a legacy of British Raj. I agree. The British had no interest other than economic exploitation. They did not bother about rural and remote areas inhabited by scheduled castes, tribes and the landless. But what have we done? The British ruled us from England from a long distance. I ask you, what are our politicians doing sitting next door at Kolkata. Don't they have eyes and ears? The governments after government in Bengal have been concentrating their efforts only on the city of Kolkata at the cost of others. We cannot accept this anomaly; we can no longer tolerate differential treatment and have to come out in the open. Do you see my point?"

"I do," said Raghavan. "The imbalance in development is not good for our country."

"Some people blame us for violent means. I am sure that you do know how it began at Naxalbari. It was the last resort of the landless against the atrocities of the landlords. The poor people had to fend for themselves and because of their resolve, they were successful. That was way back in 1967. Since then our movement has grown considerably and we have become a force to reckon with. From Bengal, the movement has spread to Jharkhand, Chattisgarh, Bihar, Orissa, Madhya Pradesh, Maharashtra and Andhra Pradesh. We have consolidated our position in the Red Corridor."

In four weeks time the wound of Bhanu had healed and he was in a position to traverse a few steps. Raghavan told him that it would take another four weeks for him to run about and resume his work.

Bhanu kept on talking about the importance of Naxal movement and the doctor listened to him patiently. Raghavan remembered the prediction made by the Guruji and his advice. He was very cautious and did not utter any word to annoy Bhanu. In the evenings he thought about the day's proceedings. The Naxal leader was right when he talked about imbalance in development and large tracts of areas being left out. However, the doctor did not approve terrorism or violence of any kind. Violence was resort of those leaders who lacked the ability to organise mass movement. They did not come out in the open and operated from God forsaken areas which lacked administration. Such movements drained the resources of the country and delayed development. The picture that Bhanu painted was one sided and did not address the problem in totality. Raghavan did not ask him any question on their organisation, source of arms supply and financial backing. He did not get into any argument.

Meanwhile, Sunil Chatterjee and Vijayan Nambudri were getting weekly mail from Raghavan. They did not contain any information other than his health. Vijayan spoke to Mamata and her father and told them that the *kundalis* were matching. The Guruji was firm that nothing would happen to Raghavan and the marriage would take place within two months. That was a happy forecast and Mamata kept her fingers crossed.

A few days later, during the routine medical visit of the doctor, Bhanu asked-

"Are you writing letters to your parents?"

"Yes, once a week without fail."

"But you do not know if your letters reach them. Also, you do not know how they are. There is no way for them to communicate with you. Well, I have made enquiries. They are fine. I thought I should tell you this."

Raghavan thanked him for the foresight and gesture. He had not spoken to anyone for the last six weeks.

"I have taken a great liking for you. You are good in your profession and it is not only me but the whole lot whom you have been treating are full of praise for you. We have been getting doctors here before, but you are the best that we have come across."

Raghavan said, "The patients are the best judges of doctors."

Bhanu continued, "Our movement is doing well but sometimes I become pensive and get into doubts. You see, the success of any movement depends on the quality of leaders and that is our weak point. So far our achievements have been good but that was because we did not get much of resistance. We can manage ordinary police force and keep them at bay but not the army. Our political wing has been able to prevail upon the government not to deploy armed forces against us. We have been able to convince them that we should not be treated like enemy. But if paramilitary forces are trained, they would be as good as the regular army. The government has already started training these forces. I do not know if we would be able to meet this new challenge. I have been warned to go for an assignment to train junior leaders. The people are with us but if leadership fails, they will look the other way."

"That is true," said Raghavan. "I heard on TV that the government besides the training of paramilitary forces is planning to earmark more funds for the development of backward regions. What would you do if that happens?"

"If that happens, we are the winners. That's what we have been fighting for. But the problem of development would not end there. The affected people must be consulted and involved in the development of their region. We will have to ensure that funds are correctly utilised and not laundered in corruption."

"Corruption is a big problem," said the doctor. "I recall Anatole France- anyone who gets into power becomes corrupt. Misuse of funds in activities like education, religion and sports is most irritating. People have lost the sense of dedication. We need to illumine and enlighten our minds."

Bhanu laughed. "Illumination and enlightenment of mind which you are talking about was lost in *Satyug*[1]. In our days we need strict and stringent measures backed by harsh punishments. We alone can do it because of our ideology."

In their next meeting, Bhanu told the doctor that he had received orders to go to Chattisgarh for the training of comrades. He has to reach there in a fortnight's time.

"Tell me if I would be fit by that time."

"You will be OK but go slow for a month or two."

"You know Raghavan, I will miss you most. Living under these conditions I do not get any opportunity to talk to intellectuals like you. You have not only cured me but also given me company for the last six weeks. Tell me, what can I do for you?"

"I have no crib in staying here but there is one thing which perturbs me."

"What's that?"

"Look, I belong to a fairly orthodox Brahmin family. We

1. The age of truth.

believe in horoscopes. I have to get married before this Durga Puja."

"That is not far off. Barely a month is left. Normally we keep doctors for six months at a time. But in your case due to the peculiar problem of yours, you must be released as soon as possible. Have your parents decided upon the girl?"

"Yes, it is all fixed up," said Raghavan.

"My friend, now leave it to me. I will see to it that you are released before I leave this camp; thereafter you take care of yourself."

"Can I inform them? They would be happy and would start making preparations. They don't have much time."

"No. Your letter will be censored and you will get into trouble. But I see your point; I will ensure that they get a hint. You see, due to security reasons even I am not allowed to speak openly."

Ten days later in the evening Bhanu went to the hut of the doctor. He told him to get ready. A van was going to Kolkata and he would be dropped there.

It was their last meeting. Bhanu hugged Raghavan. Emotional as he was, tears rolled down his eyes.

"I wonder if I will ever meet a selfless, dedicated person like you."

"It applies equally to you. We are in different professions but common to us is sincerity to life."

Bhanu wished a long and happy married life to his friend. "I would not be able to attend your wedding but my best wishes will always be with you."

"I would not like this to be the end of our friendship," said Raghavan. "Let me know whenever you have time. I will come and meet you and believe me I will keep it as secret."

"I do not know when that opportunity will come but if I am wounded again you must come and treat me. I am leaving this camp tomorrow for the new location."

There was a forced smile on Bhanu's face. The van had

come to pick Raghavan. They hugged again and parted company. Bhanu told his friend to take care.

It was four thirty in the morning when Sunil Chatterjee heard the sound of the call bell. He went to the door and peeped through the hole. It was Raghavan. Quickly he opened the door and welcomed his prospective son-in-law.

Sunil and his wife were very happy to see Raghavan. He looked about the same except for the loss of weight. Without losing time Mamata was contacted and their talk went on for a long time. He also spoke to his father.

Raghavan narrated the story from abduction to release. He was feeling tired. After a heavy breakfast he went to sleep. Mamata rang up after an hour. Her father told her that he was sleeping and she should not disturb him. She rang up again after another hour only to hear rebuke from her father.

Raghavan woke up after four hours. He shaved, had leisurely bath and was ready to go to his apartment and the college. Mr Chatterjee told him that it might not be possible.

"Why?"

"You have to take the flight for Thiruvanthapuram. Your father is anxious to meet you. You have only three hours available to you."

"I too am keen to meet him but why is there a frantic hurry?"

"Your father is not keeping well."

"He didn't tell me that."

"I suppose he did not want to put you in worries, but surely Mamata must have told you that."

"She didn't."

"She is such a forgetful girl and right now she must be lost with so many things on, in her mind. You know, when you were sleeping she rang up twice. May be she wanted to tell you just that. You must have a quick bite and get ready to move. Your ticket has already been purchased."

"I must inform the college that I am back."

"I will do that. Also give me the keys of your flat; I will get it cleaned."

Sunil Chatterjee with two young men went to the airport to see off Raghavan. They stayed on till the flight took off to satisfy themselves about his departure.

During the flight Raghavan was not feeling happy with the way he was packed off from Kolkata. He felt like an errant boy being sent to the parents by the school authorities. He had spoken to his father and could not believe that he was all that serious. People were flapping unnecessarily.

At Thiruvanthapuram Raghavan's parents came to receive him. The car in which he was travelling was escorted by police jeeps in the front and rear. He was driven to his cousin's house who was Deputy Commissioner of Police. Raghavan felt awkward; he asked his father—

"What is all this security about?"

"We are taking precaution."

"Against what?"

"You were kidnapped by the Naxals. We are not going to take any chance."

Raghavan laughed. "I was not abducted for ransom money, enmity or any such thing. They needed a doctor and they got one. I was in no way ill treated."

"That part is OK but the period of caution is not yet over. Not many days are left and therefore I am taking utmost precaution. And remember that you have also got to get married."

"What have you planned for me?"

"You go to America as soon as possible. There you will be out of the harm's way."

"I was told by Mr. Chatterjee that you are not keeping well. How are you feeling?"

"Not well. I look calm and composed but inside me the

worries were eating me. Now that you are before me, I am feeling much better. The worries will not leave me till such time you reach a safe haven. I am glad that you came here straight.

Raghavan stayed for a week at Thiruvanthapuram with his cousin in the security area. He did not move out anywhere. His parents were with him all the time. Meanwhile the flight formalities were completed and he was seen off to US.

The next few days for Mamata and Raghavan were not only happy but also hectic. They were the Puja days and their marriage had to be solemnised before it was over.

Raghavan was telling Mamata how quickly his last three weeks had passed from the time of disclosure to Bhanu regarding his impending marriage. He told her about the friendship he had developed and the noble side of his character. It was unfortunate that he had got involved in the Naxal movement.

"But tell me, why was such a hush-hush created for my travel? There was no danger to my life!"

"That is what you think but we were in a terrible state. Baba had received a call saying, 'the consignment will be reaching you shortly; start preparations and take care.' The caller hung up abruptly and Baba could not ascertain any details. He rang me up and your father. Since then we were on conference call every day. We made out that the word consignment pertains to you but we could not comprehend the meaning of start preparations and take care. Do you know we really got upset, terribly scared? Your father suggested that your movements should be kept as secret. You should not meet anyone and move out from Kolkata as soon as possible."

Raghavan smiled. "Actually I had told Bhanu to send your father a message regarding my impending release. That would have given him more time for preparation of wedding arrangements. I thought that the marriage would take place in Kolkata; that was what you wanted. Bhanu told me that he cannot speak openly but he will send a hint. As far as 'take care' is concerned it was just his habit, a pet phrase and nothing else. I now understand why your Baba did not allow me to go to the flat and the college."

"That's correct. All this is OK but I tell you that those were the most miserable days."

Raghavan smiled. "OK. Gone is gone and let's forget it. The consignment is right in front of you; what do you want to do with it?"

She pulled him close and embraced Raghu with kisses.

Mamata had made arrangements for the marriage. Her friend Sharmila had shifted to New Jersey which had a large population of persons of Indian origin. She had taken upon the responsibility to organise marriage. She told Mamata that the Indians in that place had modernised and to them it was a routine; the priests performed marriages in a businesslike manner. They did not care about *muhurt*[1] and performed only the essential Vedic rites. All that Mamata and her fiancé were required to do was to reach that place a day earlier. Nonetheless, Mamata had checked up from Raghu's father. He had said that *Dashmi*[2] would be the most auspicious day.

"And when is that?"

"Day after."

1. Auspicious date and time.
2. Tenth day of Durga Puja.

SHANTA BABU

Shanta Babu was well known in the town for various reasons: the sporting crowd admired him for his game of hockey, he was their best left forward with maximum number of goals to his credit; in the club and social circles he was a debonair who charmed others because of his looks, manners and speech; the poor people respected him for his philanthropic activities and the men of religion liked him for his simplicity and adherence to all codes and customs. In all these activities he was helped by the financial situation in which he was placed. Babu Brothers were the richest family of Gorakhpur.

I remember him from my childhood days. I was around 14 years in age and he a tall and handsome man of 35 years. My mother, separated from her husband, had run into legal difficulties. She needed power of attorney and a pleader to fight her case in the court. I vividly recall his immediate response for help. "Don't worry; it is a simple case, my *Vakil*[1] will do the needful." My mother was grateful and asked him for a cup of tea. He declined the offer and said with a smile that he would come for meals after completion of work. Shanta Babu had no inhibitions in meeting people of lower class and status. A few weeks later he came to our house with his wife for a simple meal.

1. Lawyer.

I still remember going around in his sports model car. That was the only car in Gorakhpur of its type in nineteen forties. His house was like a palace in 5 acres of land. I became his admirer and craved that I should become something like him when I grew up. There was one thing which I did not know at that age; Shanta Babu had numerous problems to cope up.

His major problems were within the family. His elder brother Kanta Babu was senior to him by fifteen years and was head of the joint family. Kanta Babu was not keeping good health due to various ailments and remained within the four walls of the house. He had a son and a daughter. The daughter was happily married; his son was causing anxiety. He was lazy and not good in studies. Kanta and Shanta Babu were looking forward to the next generation to take over the business responsibility and that was becoming doubtful. The trouble started after the marriage of Gaurav. He had married the daughter of a government pleader. Vakil Sahib incited his son in-law for greater share of money.

Kanta and Shanta Babu got along well like two brothers. They had brought up the inherited family business; first it was Kanta and now it was Shanta's turn. Every fortnight Shanta used to show the accounts to his elder brother and seek his advice.

"All this is OK," said the elder brother, "but a problem has come up which we have to solve."

"What's that?"

"Gaurav wants to start a business."

"That's good. I am glad he is showing interest. How much money does he need?"

"Ten lakhs."

Shanta thought for a while. He calculated liquid assets and loan that he could muster and concluded that the amount could be raised. Gaurav lacked business acumen but that won't matter; they had good managerial staff who would take care. The requirement was for the new generation to come forward.

He told his elder brother that the money could be managed.

Kanta Babu had a hearty laugh and called his brother near to him. He stroked his head with affection. Shanta Babu was feeling awkward.

"*Babua*[1], the thing is not that simple. You do understand that we have money and there are people who have an eye on it. Gaurav does not want his scheme to be a part of Babu Brothers Ltd. He is aspiring for independent business."

"How would he manage that?"

"Exactly, but he thinks he can. I asked him about the details but he does not disclose it. He wants to keep it as a secret."

"That is strange," said Shanta Babu.

"Did you say, strange? It is a case of deliberate mischief and planned villainy. You know Gaurav, he is a simpleton, not very clever but he certainly is not a scoundrel. Behind his actions there is a crook and I have identified him. It is his father in-law, the Vakil Sahib; that *kayastha*[2] is instigating him and firing from his shoulders."

"Vakil Sahib does not have a good reputation. Strangely, his daughter is a good girl."

"Yes, Sunanda is a sweet and good girl. I don't think that she is involved but one can never be sure."

Shanta assured his elder brother that he would go into the problem in a discreet manner and find a solution. Kanta stressed that the seed of discord had been sown and they must tread cautiously.

Gorakhnath temple is the most revered place in Gorakhpur. The *Mahant*[3] of the temple had always been a powerful figure regarded by the people in highest esteem. Shanta Babu went to the temple to seek his advice.

Mahant knew Babu Brothers well. The latter were generous

---

1. Affectionate name.
2. Caste associated with script writhing.
3. High priest.

in offering help for the upkeep of the temple premises. He advised Shanta Babu to remain cool; such incidents are common in almost all big families. He told Shanta Babu about the famous line of Tulsidas; '*Janh sampati tanh vipati nana.*[1]' Mahant advised Shanta Babu to offer prayers on four successive Tuesdays at *Hanumangarhi*[2] and thereafter perform *pooja*[3] of *Satya Narayan*[4].

Shanta Babu told his wife Nalini about the problem being created by Gaurav and his desire to start an independent business.

"That would amount to a breakup of the joint family," said Nalini.

"Exactly and we have to avert that."

"I am baffled. Is Sunanda provoking her husband?"

"I don't know. *Bade bhayya*[5] is having doubts on Vakil Sahib."

"That may be so but you can never trust girls. She was married just a year ago. Gaurav is infatuated by her and hardly moves out of the bedroom. It looks to me that she has started playing feminine tricks."

"If it is so, there would be noticeable change in her behaviour. Have you observed anything unusual in her?"

"No."

"I suggest you keep a watch on her and let me know if anything abnormal strikes your mind. Her maid servant may also reveal some information."

Nalini did as she was told. At the end of every week she informed her husband about the developments. There was no change in Sunanda's behaviour. The maid servant did not report any thing abnormal.

Four weeks had passed.

---

1. Wherever there is wealth, there are numerous troubles.
2. The temple of Hanuman.
3. Worship.
4. Lord Vishnu.
5. Elder brother.

Satya Narayan Katha[1] was organised on a grand scale. Sunanda was taking keen interest. She felt that it was being held for prosperity in her married life after completion of one year. The entire household and visitors had gathered to hear *Katha* in the evening. Gaurav was not to be seen.

Nalini asked, "Where is your husband?"

"*Choti Ma*[2], he is not feeling well. His stomach is upset."

"What's gone wrong with him?"

"Gases and bloated stomach."

"That should not be a problem." Nalini went to her room to fetch a bottle of Gelusil. She told Sunanda to give a tablespoon of antacid with a glass of water.

When Sunanda went to her room she found Gaurav seated on a reclining chair, rubbing his belly with hands. She gave him the medicine and told him that she would be back after half an hour.

Katha had started. Sunanda got engrossed and forgot to look up her husband. She was surprised to see him at the *katha* site clad in *kurta and dhoti*[3]. He was wearing a smile on his face.

The two brothers and their wives were happy to see Gaurav. He was the eldest boy of the next generation.

After dinner the husband and wife were in a relaxed mood. Gaurav told his wife that there was a letter for her from her father. Vakil Sahib wants the letter to be signed by you and returned to him as early as possible.

'What's the letter about?"

"I don't know, I haven't read it."

Sunanda took the letter and after reading, she burst out in laughter.

"What's so funny?"

---

1. Ceremony for recital of the tale of Satya Narayan.
2. A respectful name. Here it refers to Shanta Babus wife.
3. Indian dress.

"The letter, you must read it. It says that I am being harassed by my in-laws; my living in the house has become hazardous, and I and my husband want to live separately."

Gaurav took the letter. It was a long letter giving details of ill-treatment.

Sunanda said, "I don't know how this letter has been originated. I am not being ill-treated; on the contrary everyone in the house loves me."

Gaurav said, "It has nothing to do with good or bad treatment. Your father is working on a well thought out plan for separation from the joint family. He is preparing ground. He told me that we are losing money. I should get a minimum of ₹ 5000 per month instead of ₹ 1000 that I am getting now."

Sunanda gave him a curious look. She wanted to know details. "That part is interesting. What is he working on?"

"If we separate from the joint family we would be a big gainer. According to him I should get Rs. 10 lakhs. With that we can start our own business. We would not be dependent on any one. And it will benefit our children in the long run."

"What kind of business do you have in your mind?"

"Oh, we can start any business. The important thing is to have capital. Well, we can open a cinema hall, start motor repair workshop, construct buildings for hire, buy farmland etc, etc. You know, money begets money."

"Who is going to run around and work? Would you be able to do that?"

"I don't have to. I am going to be the financier; I will hire managers and workers."

"What if the business fails and we lose money?"

"Why should we? The employees have to work to earn their bread. Now look, some risk has to be taken. Your father told me to have two or three business activities running simultaneously. It is not possible that all of them fail at the same time."

"What about bitterness in the family?"

"There is going to be no bitterness. Our relationship will continue as before. We are opening a new branch and that is about all. I am not doing anything unusual; this practice is common in big business houses."

Sunanda kept quiet.

"Are you going to sign the letter?"

"Let me think. I will tell you tomorrow morning."

During the night Sunanda had enough time to think. She knew her father well; she felt intrigued about thorough brainwashing of her husband. He had convincing answers to all questions. In a year's time she had judged her husband; he was indeed a simpleton. He had no vices; he did not drink, smoke or gamble. His weak points were that he was an introvert, bone-lazy and did not stir out of the house. He lacked energy and acumen to be entrepreneur.

Next morning she talked to her husband.

"How well do you know my father?"

"You should know him better."

"Of course I do. Look, it is not a good thing to say bad things about one's father but much against my wish I have to. You wouldn't know details; he did not treat my mother well and I have seen it from my childhood. He extracted a big dowry for my brother's marriage and for that my *bhabhi's*[1] father had to sell his land. In money matters, he is miserly and greedy; he has cheated many of his clients and I have a feeling that he will swindle your money."

"You should have told this to me before."

"The occasion never arose."

"It has become rather late. I have already talked to my father. Well, that can be resolved but what will your father say? I do not know what to do."

"Have you committed anything to my father?"

"No. He has been talking to me for the last three months and I have been listening. You know my habit; when people

1. Brother's wife.

talk to me I say *'jee.*[1]*'* If they take it as my consent it is their interpretation."

"In that case the solution is simple. I am not going to sign the letter and that's the end."

"Your father will keep on pestering me. What should I do?"

"Just keep saying *jee*. There is something which puzzles me. If you want to open a new line of business, you could yourself talk to your father. Why was his advice required?"

"You have a point. It never occurred to me."

The house of Babu Brothers at Miranagar had two independent portions for the two brothers with separate entries. On Sunday mornings, the two families used to get together for leisurely meals.

Kanta Babu told his younger brother, "Thank God the problem has been solved. I had told you that Sunanda is a good girl, we should be grateful to her."

"The credit equally goes to Gaurav for listening to her."

Shanta Babu briefed his elder brother about the state of accounts. There was a balance of 3 Lakhs in the bank. He was thinking of opening a cinema house and appointing Gaurav as manager.

Kanta Babu said, "Will he be able to..."

"That should not be a problem. We will provide him reliable staff and involve Sunanda."

"I have faith in that girl but will she accept that responsibility?"

"We can find out."

Gaurav and Sunanda were called. Kanta Babu told them about the proposal made by his younger brother. He told his son that it was time that he should start taking interest in the family business. He told Sunanda to give helping hand. He asked them their views.

---

1. A passive ejaculation by the listener.

Gaurav said, '*Jee*.'

Sunanda laughed. "Don't say *Jee*; say that you accept the offer." Gaurav smiled and did that. Sunanda told her in-laws that she would get the opportunity of seeing films and she would assist her husband. Shanta Babu said that the job would carry a monthly salary of ₹ 5000. Gaurav felt happy.

Kanta Babu was pleased with the way the problem was handled by his younger brother. Shanta Babu wanted a permanent solution; Gaurav should never again think of separation.

I completed my education from the Government Jubilee High School and St Andrews College, Gorakhpur. I got a job in Pune. No longer was I able to maintain contact with the place that had made deep impression on my mind during my childhood and young years. However, I kept on enquiring about that place and looked forward to anyone who could keep me acquainted with the latest.

Gorakhpur is situated on the banks of River Rapti. The river has a notorious name for floods and in that year it was unprecedented. A large area of the town was affected and low lying areas around Hanumangarhi temple were submerged. The Mahant of Gorakhnath told Shanta Babu to organise relief camps. The latter took the task seriously and for a month he worked day and night for the noble cause. The floods receded in due course. People were grateful to him; the local newspapers praised his work and the municipality acknowledged his efforts.

Mahant was pleased. He told Shanta Babu to stand for the elections in the State assembly. He was elected by a wide majority; the backing of Mahant played a decisive role.

The next five years were rewarding for Shanta Babu. He made an exhibition hall, acquired an agency for motor vehicles, and started a workshop for repairs and a petrol pump. His daughter and two sons were doing well in the school and the family was in good health.

However, this very period of five years was not happy for Kanta Babu. They were getting old and the health was deteriorating. But that was not something which perturbed them. Six years had passed after the marriage and Sunanda did not conceive. *Bari Ma*[1] often complained, what's the use of riches if there is no progeny?

Gaurav had started taking interest in the business and his wife was a pleasant company at work. Sunanda had exerted a good influence on him and he had become out going. They started enjoying holidays and outings, travelling to distant places. But that apart, they also missed the absence of offspring. They consulted many doctors but that did not help. They visited temples at Kashi, Prayag and Haridwar. Sunanda conceived in the seventh year and it brought joy to the whole house. The happiness did not last long; the child born was spastic. The agony was deeper. Sunanda was told that she would not be able to conceive again. Somehow she swallowed the pain but Gaurav gave up. He started drinking.

Kanta Babu and Bari Ma were irretrievably saddened. They stopped speaking and neglected to take medicines. Six months later both of them died on the same night.

Shanta Babu performed the last rites for his elder brother while Gaurav remained inebriated and did not move out of his room.

Shanta Babu felt aggrieved by the death of his elder brother and his wife but he controlled himself. He was more concerned about Gaurav; he was drinking too much. His digestion had gone bad and he had developed pain in the abdomen. The doctors told Shanta Babu that Gaurav was showing symptoms of cirrhosis and he must completely stop drinking. That was easy to say but how was he going to implement that? Sunanda felt that she was responsible for the tragedy in the house and

1. A respectful name. Here it refers to Kanta Babu's wife.

would not open her mouth. She even suggested that Gaurav should marry again to beget a healthy child.

The business was doing well and everything was normal in his family, and yet Shanta Babu was not happy. He did not want an end to his elder brother's branch of Babu family. He paid special attention to Gaurav and Sunanda.

After the demise of his elder brother, Shanta Babu used to go for regular visits to Gaurav and Sunanda in the mornings and evenings. He used to take the spastic boy in his lap and play with him. On one morning when he was playing with the child, a telephone call came and he had to leave in a hurry. Sunanda was in the kitchen. He placed the child in the lap of Gaurav and went away to take the call. When he came back, he saw a reprehensible scene. Gaurav had vomited and the stinking fluid had smeared the child's body and face. The boy was shrieking.

Sunanda came out running from the kitchen. She took away the child and got busy in cleaning him. Gaurav felt ashamed and looked towards his uncle and wife. Shanta Babu did not say even a word.

Gaurav felt humiliated and did not drink during the day. In the evening when Shanta Babu came, he apologised for the incident. The uncle said that in their family no one advises or admonishes others. It is for the individuals to exercise self control. He reminded him that he was the next senior and should something happen to him; the entire responsibility would fall on Gaurav's shoulders. He told him about the opinion of doctors to give up drinking completely.

After Shanta Babu left, Gaurav told Sunanda, "It did not occur to me that should something happen to uncle, I will have to manage the family affairs."

Sunanda said, "To run a joint family, it needs tremendous sense of responsibility and attachment. Do you realise that ever since the death of *Bade Babu and Ma*[1], Shanta Babu has been

1. Kanta Babu and his wife.

visiting us regularly? Not only that, he has been playing with and fondling our child. How many will do that?"

Gaurav realised his mistake and gave up alcohol. In six month's time he was back to normal.

Shanta Babu was magnanimous. Vakil Sahib and his son were not getting along. A few years after the marriage, the son shifted to another house and Vakil Sahib was left alone with his wife. In the mellow years the old man realised his mistakes but by then it was too late. Nemesis had struck him and he was swallowing the bitter fruits of *karma*[1]. He was inflicted by cancer and even Sunanda was not very keen to meet him. Shanta Babu corrected her and he took her along with him whenever he went to meet Vakil Sahib. The treatment of cancer was expensive; Shanta Babu came to their help and paid the bills.

Gorakhpur was developing fast, more than any other city in U.P. It had become zonal headquarters for the railways, it was connected by broad gauge line and airport had become functional. A university had come into existence and the place attracted industrial activity both from public and private sector. Kasiya attracted tourists from Buddhist countries. The statue of reclining Buddha is a marvel, the only one of its kind and a centre of attraction.

Somehow Baba Gorakhnath had not made the desired impact on people outside Gorakhpur. It did not acquire the reputation of being one of the holy cities to attract pilgrims. One day it will. However, the people of Gorakhpur hold the saint in highest esteem and the Mahants were continuing with the tradition.

Shanta Babu's political party had come into power in the state. The chief minister offered him a ministerial berth which he declined due to his involvement in the family affairs. His daughter and sons were school going and he wanted to give

1. Philosophy of action.

them personal attention.

In good time, Shanta Babu had made new additions to his inherited business and they were doing well.

I have not been to Gorakhpur for the last twenty five years nor have I met anyone from that place. I am itching for information.

I am sitting in the lawn of Pune Golf Course. It is a good course and I take hats off to those who developed it. Pune, like all other places in the plateau region, has black soil unsuitable for growing grass. Golf courses need alluvial soil and plenty of water. Pune lacks both and yet the course is good with greenery around.

The table next to me is occupied by a young couple and an elderly man. They had finished the game and were cooling their throats with coke. The man was telling the young couple about Gorakhpur. He looked like someone known to me; I glanced at him several times but could not identify him. I could not hold myself for long and I walked to his table.

"Are you from Gorakhpur?"

"Yes."

"So am I. My name is Ravi Sharma."

The man got up immediately and embraced me. "I am Sunil, Shanta Babu's son."

"It is such a great pleasure to meet you after forty years."

Sunil had married his daughter to an air force officer posted at Lohegaon. He had come to meet them. Our meeting was a great coincidence. I was keen to know all about Gorakhpur and to my luck I met the son of Shanta Babu. I invited him for dinner.

Sunil came alone in the evening. His son in-law and daughter were required to attend a function followed by dinner. He had all the time for gossip. He looked much like his father, tall and fair with sharp features but more than anything else, his voice resembled that of Shanta Babu.

"I have not met you people for a long, long time. I am keen to know all about Babu Family."

"From where should I begin?"

"The last news that I heard was that Gaurav had started drowning himself in drinks. Later I was told that he gave up drinking and was back to normal life."

"Yes, he did and that was a great relief to everyone. You see, Gaurav *Bhayya* was not a mixing type and generally he remained aloof but he was a well meaning, clean heart. He died 15 years ago."

"What about his wife, Sunanda?"

"*Bhabhi* is a noble person, great in her own ways. She looked after the spastic child in motherly manner until his death. She was a great help to my father and right now she is eldest in the family. She did something which has been very beneficial to the Babu Family."

"What was that?"

"She had employed a whole time nurse to look after the spastic child. The nurse was exceptionally well behaved and thoroughly dedicated. She was a widow and had three school going sons. Sunanda took the responsibility of their education. The boys were good and appeared to be promising. Gaurav *bhayya* also liked them.

One day she asked my father if she could adopt them. Without any hesitation, he said go ahead. He wanted continuity in Kanta Babu's branch of the family.

The three boys— Naveen, Rajesh and Pradip started living in the house. Soon they acquired the behavioural traits of an established family. They were good in studies; Naveen did graduation in law, Rajesh in business administration and Pradip in engineering. They were absorbed in our family business. My father needed reliable hands and they were most loyal. The youngest one turned out to be a brilliant boy; he started a new venture in the name of Babu Builders and that business is doing extremely well.

The adoption of three boys was a boon to our family. My father had gone old and at 75 he needed help and respite."

"Tell me about your father. He was my role model."

"Shanta Babu died last year at the age of 94."

"I didn't know that! Was he sick?"

"No. He was hale and hearty right up to the last day. After dinner, he complained about pain in the chest and in no time he died of a massive heart attack."

"I am glad that he did not suffer long years of chronic ailments like his elder brother, Kanta Babu."

"Yup, in that way he was lucky. The people of Gorakhpur remembered his services and gave him a befitting farewell. His funeral was attended by the Mahant, mayor and other dignitaries. Do you recall the big *Chowk*[1] near our house?"

I nodded.

"Well, that square has been named after him. Sunanda got a statue made from a renowned sculptor from Allahabad and that has been installed in his memory."

"Shanta Babu was a great man. I clearly remember my first meeting with him when he helped my mother."

"It was ingrained in his nature to help others. He was very fond of the family and did not like discord. He helped Kanta Babu, Gaurav and even Vakil Sahib. But unfortunately, he had to see bad blood amongst his own sons. That was the saddest part. I am one of the culprits, I admit that, but it couldn't be helped."

"What happened?" I enquired.

"You see, I and my elder brother Mahesh just could not pull on. We were OK in the childhood days but as we grew up the discord manifested itself in diverse ways. He did not like my face and used to rebuke me for something or the other."

"What was the reason?"

"I wish I could tell you that. Maybe I was bright in studies and he was a dunce. May be that my parents liked me more and may be that he felt that the family business would pass on to me

1. Crossing, square.

and not him. I can't really say but I know for certain that he had developed a kind of allergy towards me. He could not tolerate my presence. He was very short tempered and abusive.

I was sent to Germany for higher studies. He used to be quite happy during my absence. I told my father that in the interest of harmony, I should work and remain abroad. My father agreed reluctantly.

I had been visiting Gorakhpur on vacations and during those days he reverted back to his old ways and made my and everyone's life miserable. He started another row. He did not like the three boys adopted by Sunanda. He told my father that they do not have the blood of Babu Family and should be thrown out of the house. He cannot accept the sons of a maid servant as his brothers.

My father got hold of a good lawyer to convince Mahesh that what Sunanda had done was perfectly legal, within her rights. It's a different thing if he does not like them but nothing can be done in the court of law. All that he could do was to sever relationship and that he did. He forbade their entry into our wing of the house.

Around that time, Mahesh got married. His attention was diverted for sometime but thereafter he started another stunt. He told Shanta Babu that he in full picture of the business, he is male member and therefore he should become *karta*[1] of the undivided family. It should be implemented at an early date because of father's old age. This was not acceptable to my father and he decided to remain *karta* as long as possible. Mahesh was clever; he did not want the joint family to break, his desire was to take complete control of the family business as soon as possible and keep me out. He knew that after Babuji, it would be his turn. In the worst case he was prepared to wait.

You see, these were the kind of irritants which my father faced in his late years. Meanwhile my mother died and *Babuji*[2]

---

1. Head of Hindu Undivided Family.
2. A respectful name for elders. Here it refers to Shanta Babu.

was left alone. He did not feel comfortable in his portion of the house with Mahesh around and spent most of his time with Sunanda. I tell you, Mahesh was my brother but he was very mean; he started suspecting illicit relationship between my father and Sunanda. I do not know what kind of a man he was; he could not live peacefully with anyone including his own wife and children.

I wish my father had got a better treatment in his old age but that was not to be. I was away and could not be of any help."

"Did he complain?"

"No, never. He was a strong character. He eschewed nonsense stoically. He never complained to anyone but might have told bitter facts to Sunanda. She understood him well; she too had gone through the school of suffering.

But life is strange. What he could not achieve throughout his life occurred in the Babu Family soon after his death. It was a miracle which can occur only because of the blessings of Baba Gorakhnath."

"What was that?"

"Mahesh died two months after my father. That has put an end to all our problems. Our house, never before, has seen such harmony and happiness."

"That's good. I am sure you will keep it up."

"Of course, I will. I have inherited a clean slate and I have to follow my father's example."

It was getting late. We had a quiet dinner. Sunil was preparing to leave. Before going, he invited me to Gorakhpur. I promised him that I will do that.

●●●